RIKA RISING

THE GENEVIAN QUEEN – BOOK 1

BY M. D. COOPER

Thanks to the Aeon 14
Just in Time (JIT) & Beta Readers

Timothy Van Oosterwyk Bruyn
Scott Reid
Gareth Banks
Chad Burroughs
Constance Beebe
Steven Blevins

ISBN 978-1-64365-031-9

Version 1.0.0

Cover Art by Tek Tan
Editing by Jen McDonnell, Bird's Eye Books

TABLE OF CONTENTS

FOREWORD

If you've read prior Aeon 14 books, it's likely that you'll have run into Rika. She's had a novella, two short stories, and eight novels written about her (including this one). She's also shown up in other series, such as the Orion War.

Her mechs are some of the fiercest and most feared fighting forces in the galaxy. Forged through a decade of war, and then their people's defeat, Rika's Marauders would follow her to the gates of hell, kick them down, and clear the place out in record time.

If you've not read the Rika's Marauders series, and would like to know how Rika came to lead this elite fighting force, then I recommend you start with the book *Rika Outcast*. However, I endeavored to write this story as a new starting point in Rika's long tale, so if you want to dive in here, I think that will be alright as well.

When I first started telling Rika's tale, it was because I was curious about what story a woman in her situation would tell. A woman who was forcibly turned into a cyborg warrior (what her people call a mech) against her will.

That story grew and grew, finally becoming longer than the *Lord of the Rings* and *The Hobbit* combined. But really, that was just the beginning. Rika's tale from *Outcast* to *Conqueror* really just saw her reach her nation's former capital system, Genevia. There is so much more of her story to tell.

And, if you've made note of this book's series title, you just might know where that story will take her.

I'm looking forward to diving into this next leg of the journey with Rika, her mechs, and you. We're going to have the ride of our lives seeing where her adventure ultimately takes us.

I can promise you, it's not where you're expecting.

Michael Cooper
Danvers 2019

THE JOURNEY THUS FAR

Ten years ago, the Genevians and Nietzscheans were embroiled in a bitter war—a war that the Genevians were losing.

Though they were not technologically inferior to the Nietzscheans, the Genevians were a less war-like people, and when it came to fighting spirit, the Niets outstripped them handily. So the idea was born, in some dark corner of the Genevian government, to create a new type of soldier.... One with unwavering loyalty, and without fear: mechs.

The first mechs were little more than brains in jars, human intelligence married to a machine's strength. It was far from a new concept, just not one the Genevians had explored in their recent past.

Over the course of a few years, they improved upon their mechs, making several models with varying resemblance to their original human forms (detailed descriptions are at the end of this book). The mechs were controlled via an implant in their brain that used a system known as Discipline to ensure that the cyborgs behaved.

The reason for this was simple: Mechs were not volunteers.

Despite this, the Genevian mechs were highly effective and greatly feared by the Nietzscheans, but they were not enough to turn the tide of war, and the Genevians lost.

The mechs were scattered after the fight, some to mercenary companies, some to concentration camps, and others managing to find some honest labor.

Rika was one of the latter until she ran afoul of a loan shark and was sold at auction to the Marauders, a mercenary company consisting of former Genevian military personnel.

What could have been a terrible change of fate for her ended up becoming a blessing in disguise, as she earned her freedom, and then her own command within the Marauders.

As these events transpired in the corner of space occupied by Nietzschea and Genevia, a larger conflict was brewing. One between two massive empires: the Transcend, and the Orion Freedom Alliance. But between these empires lay the Inner Stars, and a tangled web of alliances and proxy nations began to fight the war on behalf of the Transcend and Orion.

Shortly after Rika gained command of her own company, that war came to her doorstep, and she met a woman who changed her life forever: Tangel Richards.

Tangel is the field marshal of a group known as the Scipio Alliance. This alliance of interstellar nations fights for the Transcend, and the Marauders joined their cause, spurred on by the knowledge that their hated enemy, the Nietzscheans, are a vassal nation of the Orion Freedom Alliance.

Seeing the potential in Rika, Tangel upgraded her mechs and outfitted them with improved equipment, then sent them into Old Genevia to win back their nation and crush the Nietzscheans.

Rika took on that mission with a fiery passion, leapfrogging through Old Genevia until she came to her people's former capital system, Genevia. Her rapid advance gave her an unexpected opportunity: she crossed paths with the Nietzschean emperor, who was overseeing construction of a new fleet in the system, and she seized the opportunity to strike.

In a crushing upset for the Nietzschean Empire, Rika's Marauders—aided by one of Tangel's fleets, led by Admiral Carson—defeated the Nietzschean fleet, and Rika herself killed their emperor.

Now the remains of the Nietzschean forces in the Genevia System are fleeing while Rika and her Marauders flush out the final pockets of Niets, and prepare for the next phase of their battle against the empire: an advance on their enemy's capital system.

PROMINENT CHARACTERS

Though there is a full list of all the mechs, pilots, and members of the Marauders at the end of the book, this is a listing of some of the more prominent characters and their current role in the battalion.

9th Marauder Battalion Leadership

Rika – Colonel, battalion commanding officer
Silva – Lieutenant Colonel, executive officer
Barne – Sergeant Major, command sergeant
Leslie – Captain, intelligence officer
Niki – AI, Lieutenant, operations officer

Other Key Characters

Tremon – Former Genevian President (known as Kalvin)
Constantine – Nietzschean Emperor Rika killed
Hammond – Constantine's chief military advisor
Oda – Leader of the Genevians hiding in The Refuge
Carson – ISF (Intrepid Space Force) Admiral

The Seventh Fleet, First Division

Heather (Smalls) – Captain of the *Fury Lance*
Travis – Captain of the *Republic*
Ferris – Lieutenant, commander of the *Undaunted*
Vargo Klen – Lieutenant, commander of the *Asora*
Ashley – CWO, bridge crew aboard the *Asora*

Buggsie – Lieutenant, commander of the *Capital*

MAPS

For more maps, and full-size versions, visit
www.aeon14.com/maps.

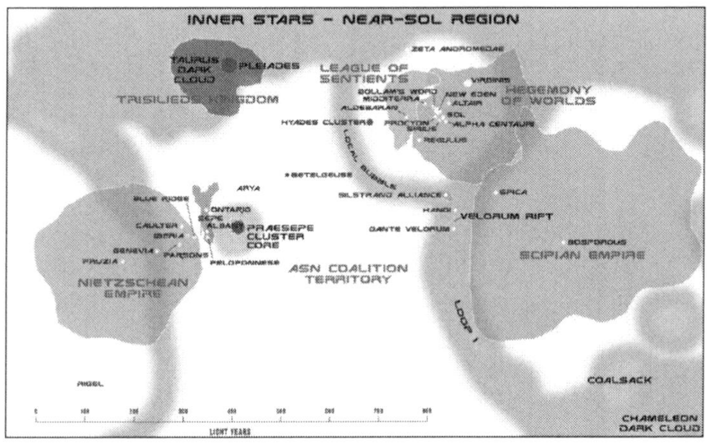

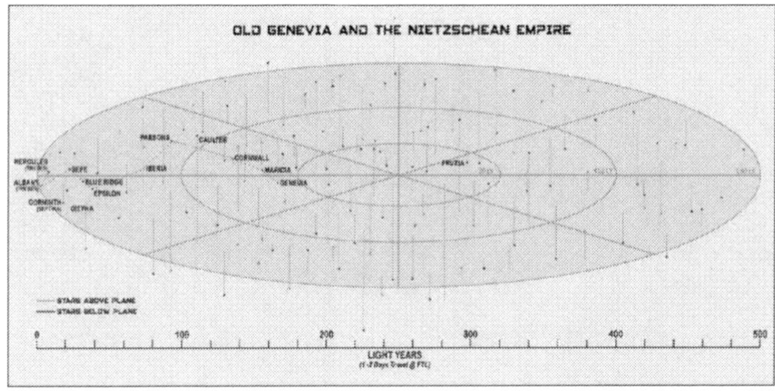

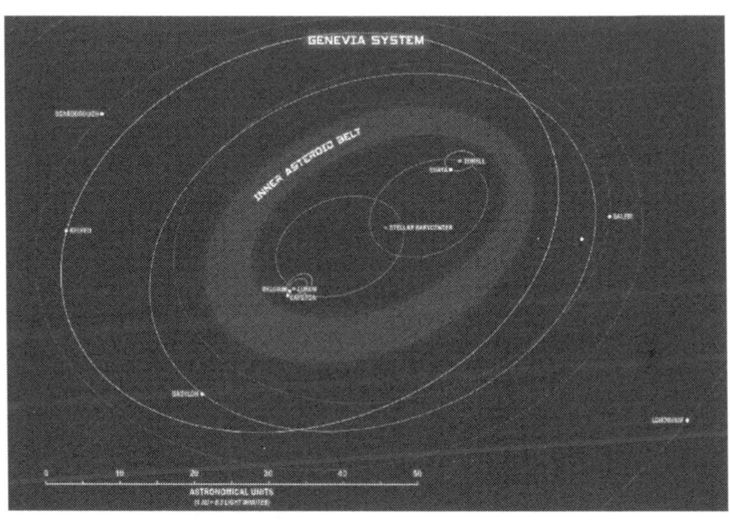
GENEVIA SYSTEM
INNER ASTEROID BELT
STELLAR BARYCENTER
0
10
20
30
40
50
ASTRONOMICAL UNITS

A NEW START

STELLAR DATE: 05.15.8950 (Adjusted Years)
LOCATION: Lisbon Station, edge of Inner Asteroid Belt
REGION: Genevia System, New Genevian Alliance

One week after the death of Emperor Constantine…

A round slammed against the bulkhead next to Rika, splashing a white-hot fluid onto the deck. She ducked back around the corner, narrowly avoiding the spray and cursing softly.

<*Heads up!*> she called out to her squad over the Link. <*Splash canisters, some sort of gelled fast-release plasma.*>

<*Well that tears it.*> Gunnery Sergeant Aaron added a few choice curses. <*Colonel, permission to bring out the big guns?*>

<*Granted, Gunny,*> Rika replied as she backed further down the corridor, retreating to an intersection where Kelly's fireteam was holding off what seemed like an unending horde of Nietzscheans swarming out of a bay sixty meters down a passage on their right.

<*Fun times that way,*> she said to the corporal, gesturing back over her shoulder to where the plasma was still glowing on the deck.

<*Heard that,*> Kelly replied.

She signaled for Shoshin to activate stealth and move across the corridor during the next break in enemy fire.

<*When do you expect that to happen, Corporal?*> the AM-4 mech asked Kelly, gesturing to the river of projectile and beam fire that was streaking down the corridor she'd directed him to cross. <*I can't even lob a 'nade without it getting shredded.*>

<*Or blowing up in your face,*> Keli added.

Rika smirked, though no one could see her face inside her helmet. <*Hold one mike. The Van is coming in.*>

<*Hell yeah!*> Keli threw a fist in the air as she switched positions with Shoshin, ready to cover him as he moved back and activated his stealth in anticipation of the break in fire.

Like Rika, Keli and Kelly were Scout Mech Infiltrator models, their slim, human bodies perfect for crafting into forward operating scouts. Shoshin was an Assault Mech model, a heavier, beefier mech that carried more firepower than the SMIs, but had less effective stealth due to his larger profile and the heat his weaponry gave off.

He spread his limbs, running a heat bleed procedure, his bulk nearly filling the narrow corridor.

While SMI mechs like Rika were smaller—averaging only two and a half meters tall, and not much wider than an armored human—AMs weren't significantly taller than SMIs, but they were wider, enough that it was often tricky for them to maneuver in smaller corridors.

Luckily, Lisbon Station was a manufacturing plant, and as such, it could easily accommodate Shoshin's size. Even better, it could accommodate The Van's.

A vibration rippled through the deck, barely noticeable at first amidst the continuous rumble of weapons fire and explosions that were shaking the station. Rika took that as her cue and clapped a hand on Kelly's shoulder before moving back to the adjacent intersection, where the plasma rounds had forced her back a minute before.

In the intervening time, more plasma canisters had hit the bulkheads and deck, melting away the surfaces with ten-thousand-degree heat. She hoped The Van wouldn't fall through the sagging steel and plas.

<*Van, watch out for structural issues at my position,*> she advised, sending him a visual of the damage.

<*You got it, Colonel. I have my a-grav on,*> the K1R mech replied.

<*Really?*> Rika queried. From the vibrations rippling through the deck, it didn't seem like it.

<*Believe it or not, he does,*> Niki, the AI embedded in Rika's mind, confirmed. <*It's the station's artificial gravity that's having trouble with several tons of Van running through at a hundred kilometers per hour.*>

<*Shit,*> Rika muttered. <*Is Lisbon taking that much of a pounding?*>

<*No, just shoddy workmanship in general,*> the AI replied. <*This place was built shortly after the war ended. Forced labor and all that.*>

<*Still wish we could have just blown it away,*> Rika muttered as she took up a position that would allow her to quickly follow in The Van's wake once he reached her location.

Niki laughed softly in Rika's mind. <*Heather is still suggesting that on the command network.*>

<*I know, I muted her unless she sends a priority message. It was annoying, and Tremon would have my head if we just started blowing away any station that resisted.*>

<*Even one swarming with Niets?*> Niki asked.

<*Well, it's more a strategic decision than a tactical one. I'd like them to surrender and show that they'll be treated well. It'll make the other holdouts easier to deal with.*>

The AI made a snorting sound. <*Rika, sometimes I think you're too soft. If you blow away one station,* ***that*** *will make the others surrender without any trouble. They're only fighting because they think they have a chance.*>

Though Niki's logic was cold and a little heartless, there was truth in it. But encouraging the surrender of the remaining Nietzschean holdouts was not Rika's only motivation. She also had to show the people of the Genevia System that she was a better ruler than the enemy.

Ruler…. The word reverberated in her mind. *Is that what I am now? Really?*

The fact that she had risen from what was virtually indentured servitude to a colonel in the Marauders, and now to the—at least currently—apparent head of the re-emerging Genevian nation was beyond surreal.

A more responsible version of Rika would be back on Belgium, seeing to matters of state, but things felt more 'right' to her when she was with her Marauders, duking it out in the corridors of some station. The work necessary to establish the New Genevian Alliance would keep—the Nietzschean holdouts wouldn't.

Rika wasn't even certain that reforming a Genevian nation was either wise or necessary. To her, it felt like a problem for five years from now, but Tremon argued that it was in Genevia's best interest to lay a solid foundation now.

Or at least argue a lot about what a solid foundation looks like.

Her thoughts were interrupted as the vibrations beneath her feet reached a crescendo, their climax punctuated by a grey blur shooting past on her right. Amidst the incoming plasma fire and the haze of the super-heated air, she almost missed that The Van was holding a thick piece of exterior hull plating, his shoulder-mounted chainguns spraying tungsten rounds over the upper edge.

Rika ducked into his wake, letting the K1R and his shield protect her from incoming fire—which was highly effective, given that his bulk nearly filled the entire passage. Her biggest worry was finding sure footing and avoiding the hot metal and plasma droplets that were falling from the overhead.

The Van's speed began to decrease as the enemy switched from plasma to kinetic rounds, rail-shots wearing away at the red-hot chunk of hull plating he held.

<*Should just fire a tacnuke at these assholes,*> he grunted.

<*Van! We're **inside** the station, remember?*>

<*I'd be fine,*> the K1R mech replied. <*And you can hide behind*

me.>

Niki laughed at The Van's nonchalance. *<You know, if we were to blow a few airlocks, the pressure wave probably wouldn't be that destructive if you dialed the yield back.>*

<Stars, what is it with everyone?> Rika asked. *<We're trying* ***not*** *to blow up the station.>*

<Your call, Colonel,> The Van replied.

Rika wondered if her Marauders were growing weary of the fighting. Major engagements in the Genevian System had ended a week ago, and now her mechs were digging enemies out of hidey holes like Lisbon Station. She knew from experience that it was a tiresome slog, both physically and emotionally. The glory had already been won, this was just dangerous cleanup work.

<Get ready to drop your shield when we get to the next intersection,> Rika advised The Van. *<The bulk of their forces will be on the left, coming out of that bay. You give them a full barrage—minus nukes—and I'll cover your six.>*

<You got it, Colonel.>

They reached the intersection a moment later. It was wider than the others—over ten meters across, a wide pentagonal space where five corridors met—and strewn with bodies from The Van's relentless assault. Only three soldiers remained alive, crouched behind a grav shield on the right.

They opened fire on The Van's unprotected flank, but the K1R didn't even slow, casually flinging the piece of hull plate at them before turning to the left and firing his six primary weapons at the Nietzscheans who were pinning down Kelly's fireteam.

The hull plate smashed through the shield and crushed one of the Niets; a series of rounds from the GNR that was Rika's right arm finished off the other two.

She sprinted to the hull plate The Van had thrown and jammed her hand beneath, heaving it upright and wedging it between a conduit riser and what looked like a sewage pipe to give her extra cover, should more enemies attack from down the other corridors.

At present, the only Niets that Rika could see were the ones The Van was firing at, but as much as she liked to watch the K1R work, she kept her focus on the other passageways, ensuring that they wouldn't be hit from the rear.

<Well, I crossed the corridor,> Shoshin announced. *<Kinda easy when The Van is melting holes in the station.>*

<This is why we don't normally deploy K1Rs in combat like this,> Captain Chase's welcome voice came over the combat net. *<How are things in your neck of the woods?>*

<Oh, you know,> Rika replied, nonchalance masking her relief. *<Same ol' grind. Glad you're back on the Link. Had us worried.>*

<Some Niets flanked us and melted the corridor our comm relay was in,> the company's CO replied. *<Took a few minutes to tap into a functional portion of the station network.>*

<I'm glad that's all it was,> Rika responded privately. *<I'd be pretty upset if you got killed in some minor skirmish.>*

The AM-4 snorted. *<But if I died in a major engagement, that would be OK?>*

<Only if it was heroic…like you were saving me, or something,> she replied. *<Then I'd cherish the memory forever.>*

<That's my plan, Rika. To go down in a blaze of glory, saving your ass. I mean…it's a great ass. Totally worth saving.>

Rika laughed and then spotted a pair of Niets moving down the middle corridor she was covering. A depleted uranium rod leapt from the muzzle of her GNR and shredded the strut they were hiding behind. Only one of the enemies retreated.

<Well,> she replied to Chase. *<I'm glad you have your priorities straight.>*

<One of us has to.>

Though his tone carried a note of amusement, she knew that he was making a veiled comment about how she shouldn't be on the ground in an engagement like this. Even in private, Chase never directly questioned her command decisions, but he did make his opinions known.

In short, he believed that her value as a leader was greater than her value as an individual combatant.

He's right, of course. What colonel deploys with frontline soldiers?

The problem Rika continually faced was that she *liked* being a soldier in the thick of things. It was so much easier, just a matter of point and shoot. Being a colonel wasn't so bad, even a colonel in command of a fleet and all the lives aboard her ships.

But a civilian leader? That was something else entirely.

<Well?> Chase asked a moment later, and Rika shook her head, startled out of her reverie.

<Well what?>

<Do you want me to send Squad Three up to your position,> he asked, not commenting on her lack of response to the question she'd missed. *<We have things in hand down here. Once you take out that detachment, there's nothing between your team and the Command Center.>*

Rika was watching feeds from Kelly and The Van as they moved into the bay where the Nietzscheans had been holed up. The weapons fire finally fell silent as at least twenty of the enemy surrendered.

<Yeah, that would be good. We've got more white flags here.>

Chase laughed. *<You sound so down about it. Isn't getting the enemy to surrender the goal?>*

<Well, the goal is to have them surrender without a fight. These asshats made a big fuss and ***then*** *gave up.>*

<A big fuss? I like that. I'm using it in my next briefing.>

Rika chuckled as she tagged the location of the Niet who had retreated down the middle corridor. *<I look forward to hearing how you work it in.>*

<That's not all I want to work in,> Chase replied, his voice laden with innuendo.

<OK, you two lovebirds,> Niki interjected. *<Can you save the sexytime talk for when we're not still in the middle of an engagement? I'd like Rika to stay frosty.>*

<I'm always frosty,> Rika replied. *<Plus, I can walk and chew gum at the same time.>*

<Prove it,> the AI challenged.

Rika pulled the hull plate free and let it fall to the deck, not wanting to leave it as cover for any enemies. She dropped a pair of sensor drones and then threaded her way through the Nietzschean corpses, following in the path of destruction The Van had wrought.

At the end of the corridor, Shoshin stood outside the bay the enemies had been spewing from, covering a pair of injured Niets while another knelt next to them, applying biofoam to their wounds.

"Hurry it up," he growled at the woman. "Soon as you get them sealed up, I want you to take your buddies into the bay."

"I can't move them," she protested. "Not till their med systems stabilize them."

Shoshin shrugged and lifted his rifle. "Then I take them out of the equation. We can't guard wounded POWs in every corridor across the station."

"Fuckin' mechs," the Nietzschean soldier grunted. "They take your heart out when they cut up your body to make you into a machine?"

"No." Shoshin shook his head. "Your people did that when you burned my homeworld. I was already missing most of the parts they cut off to make a mech by the time your people were through with me."

Rika cocked an eyebrow. Shoshin was one of the most reserved of her Marauders; he rarely spoke at all, let alone shared anything about his past. He hadn't even opted to have facial reconstruction surgery, still sporting the near-featureless and skinless face that the Genevian Armed Forces had granted him upon mechanization. She wondered what was loosening his tongue.

The Nietzschean opened her mouth to speak, but then saw Rika standing nearby and shook her head, turning her focus back to her task.

After a quick slap on Shoshin's shoulder, Rika walked into the bay to see The Van standing guard over the now two dozen Niets who had surrendered. Only a few of them were injured, and most of the others were only lightly armored.

<This an HQ company?> she asked Niki as she approached Kelly and Keli, who stood just inside the bay's entrance.

<Looks like it. I don't see a major or colonel in the mix, though. Either they're dead, or they fled.>

<Dead or fled,> Rika said with a laugh. *<I like it. I hope they ran away so they can lead their troops to defeat yet another day.>*

"So? Should we toss them all out the airlock?" Kelly asked aloud.

Keli snorted, her rifle sweeping across the group of Niets. "No worse than what they would have done to us."

"Easy now, private," Rika said as she looked over the group. "Who's senior here?"

A man held up his hand. "Captain Harl. Company intelligence officer."

"And your CO?" Rika asked. "Did he cut and run?"

The man's expression said yes, but he shook his head. "He was headed to the C&C. Probably there by now."

"I guess we'll just have to go pay him a visit," Rika said, noting that Squad Three's first fireteam was almost at the bay.

"CJ's going to be here in a minute to keep an eye on you, and then you'll get shipped off to the detention site on Capeton."

"Capeton?" one of the Niets blurted.

Keli took a menacing step toward the speaker. "Airlock's still an option."

Five minutes later, Sergeant CJ had arrived and taken custody of the POWs. With things in hand, Rika, the two Kellies, Shoshin, and The Van got on the move. They were bolstered by CJ's first squad, consisting of Yig, Goob, Cole, and Fiona.

The nine mechs moved through the station with practiced efficiency. Their internal mods fed visual overlays directly into their optical nerves, giving them multiple views of their surroundings, noting access hatches, corridors, likely places for ambush, and defensible positions.

In addition to the wealth of real-time data, the mechs of Rika's M Company had run a dozen simulated assaults on Lisbon Station while en route. While they didn't know it *quite* as well as the backs of their three-fingered hands, they weren't going to lose their way, either.

<*Think this is the last one, Colonel?*> Cole asked as they moved down a maglev track that connected the outer docking ring to the station's central spire.

<*Probably the last one for M,*> Rika replied. <*If all goes well, the other companies will take their targets in the next day or so, and the fight for Genevia will be over.*>

<*The Genevian System, at least,*> Goob qualified. <*Still a few hundred other star systems to liberate if we want to get the whole alliance back.*>

Rika nodded in response, wishing everyone wasn't constantly bringing up their priorities—especially when those priorities ran contrary to the mission she'd been given by Admiral Tangel.

The admiral had instructed Rika to keep driving until she reached the heart of the Nietzschean Empire. Just because they'd killed Emperor Constantine a week ago, didn't mean that the Niets were on their knees.

The enemy's fleet admiral, a man named Hammond, had escaped Genevia with a sizable fleet. He would make it back to Nietzschea and rally their forces for a counterattack, and at present, he had just one target to strike out at: the Genevia System. If Rika started to liberate neighboring systems, he'd be spoiled for choices, and she'd be spread thin defending those systems.

If the ISF fleet under Admiral Carson were going to remain in Genevia, things would be different, but Rika knew that the ISF ships were in high demand. Before long, they would be called to aid in one of the other battles raging across the Orion Arm of the galaxy.

No, it's my job to stop Nietzschea. Tangel entrusted me with that; I'm going to do my duty.

Rika just wasn't sure when running a nation had become a part of that duty—though it occurred to her that such responsibility might have been one of Tangel's desired side effects.

After all, she went through a similar progression. Except she's responsible for half of known space.

The thought of being in charge of what amounted to the bulk of humanity was enough to make Rika's head spin—something which did nothing to mitigate the angst she felt over being in charge of her own small corner of the Orion Arm.

<*Rika.*> Niki's voice broke through her thoughts. <*A team just spotted a Niet with oak leaves on his collar heading down to the spire's engineering section with a large detachment.*>

Rika tapped into the appropriate feeds and saw that Fred's team had made the sighting.

<*Fred, can you pursue? We're coming.*>

<*Working on it, ma'am,*> the corporal replied. <*They peeled off a whack of heavies to slow us down, though. You'd have a better chance of getting in on the action if you flank down the other side of the spire.*>

Niki pulled up the available routes, and Rika selected the best one for her team.

<*OK, Fred, give 'em hell. We're going down Shaft 3A. Looks like Alison is already bringing another team down to help you.*>

<*Saw that. Good thing, too, these Niets are fighting like there's no tomorrow.*>

The corporal's statement triggered a suspicion in Rika, and she looked over the lower decks of the station's spire.

Lisbon was a standard ring-and-spindle station: a fifteen-kilometer-long spire with six toroid rings along its length. The rings were situated at the upper end of the spire, and the central command systems, as well as the primary reactors, engines and station-keeping systems, were at the lower end.

What *wasn't* down at the lower end were ships. A few bays serviced the engineering section, but according to the logs, no vessels were currently berthed down there. Which meant that either the Nietzschean colonel had an off-the-record escape craft he was heading toward, or he had other plans.

<*Niki, are you thinking what I'm thinking?*>

The AI snickered. <*It's bad form for me to let on that I can read your mind, Rika.*>

<*What?!*> she exclaimed, worried her AI actually could, then Niki chuckled and assuaged her fears.

<*I'm kidding. You know that. But if I were a betting AI—which I sort of am, given that I'm riding around in your noggin—I'd wager that our friendly neighborhood Nietzschean colonel is going to blow the station.*>

<*Yeah, that's where I was going with it as well,*> Rika replied

before switching to the company's general combat net. *<All Marauders, be aware that the Nietzscheans may be trying to scuttle the station.>*

<You heard the colonel, and you know the drill,> Chase's voice followed a moment later. *<General alarm, move POWs to bays, direct civilians to evac pods.>*

<Blowing the horn,> Potter, the company's AI, announced.

A moment later, the station's general evac sounded on both audible systems and the Link, lights flashing every few meters on the bulkheads.

<OK, people,> Rika advised her team. *<We're on the clock now. The Niets know that we know what they're planning, so they're gonna doubletime it.>*

<Sure,> Kelly said from the head of the group. *<But do they know that we know that they know what they're planning?>*

<Shut up, Kelly,> The Van grunted.

The SMI-4 mech laughed. *<Be nice, or I'm gonna hop on your back for a piggyback ride.>*

Rika saw that The Van said something privately to Kelly, but didn't tap into the message. Whatever it was silenced the SMI-4, and there was no chatter until the team reached the shaft that would take them down to the engineering levels.

<Scouts first,> Rika ordered.

<That include you?> Kelly asked as she peered down the four-kilometer-deep shaft with Keli and Fiona queued up behind her.

<Nope,> Rika shook her head. *<**I'm** gonna ride on The Van's back.>*

<Buncha comedians,> the K1R grunted.

Kelly grabbed a handhold inside the shaft, swinging out of the way. *<OK, girls. Let's do this.>*

The other two SMI mechs moved into the shaft, its five-meter diameter easily accommodating their lithe forms. Kelly let go first, followed by Keli and then Fiona.

Lisbon Station's central spire only tugged at half a *g*, and though the three mechs only fell at sixty kilometers per hour, their forms disappeared almost immediately, thanks to their stealth armor.

Two minutes later, Kelly called up, *<Secure. But watch out for a pipe halfway down, sticking out on the far side.>*

Without prompting, Yig and Cole jumped into the shaft next, the RR-4 mechs also disappearing from sight within seconds. Rika didn't wait for them to get far before she followed after, knowing that the moment she touched down, The Van would follow. The AM-4s, Goob and Shoshin, would be last.

Advance by model was something the mechs were well versed in. They'd practiced maneuvers like this a thousand times, and everyone knew their place, regardless of the fireteam and squad they normally belonged to.

As Rika fell, she pulled visual feeds from the other SMI mechs, noting that the bottom of the shaft was a wide platform with crates stacked on one side, sitting at the edge of a two-hundred-meter open space. A dozen meters below the platform, and seventy closer to the center of the spire, was the Nietzschean's likely target: the station's power plant.

Like many stations, the primary source of power was an array of fusion reactors. Lisbon, however, also possessed an antimatter reactor. Station records showed that there were several kilograms of antimatter on hand—more than enough to blast the spire to bits and twist the toroid rings apart.

<Anything?> Rika asked the other SMIs.

<Nuffin,> Kelly replied. *<Granted, with all the tanks, pipes, conduit, fab shops and storage down here, you could tuck a battalion away and it would take a day to ferret them out.>*

Rika sent an affirmative response, continuing to watch through her team's eyes as the RR-4s touched down and spread out.

A hundred meters before she reached the bottom of the shaft, Rika activated her a-grav systems and slowed enough that the impact of her feet on the platform was no more than a muted thud, lost in the general cacophony of the cavernous space.

She moved toward Kelly's position, the SMI visible only by a marker on Rika's HUD indicating that the mech was crouched at the edge of the platform. Once there, Rika surveyed the routes that the enemy could take to reach the antimatter, which was stored in three separate locations, each accessible only via catwalk.

<*We're going to have to secure every one of those,*> she said as the platform vibrated beneath her feet, heralding The Van's touchdown.

<*We can take the one on the far side of the reactors,*> Kelly replied. <*We'll drop relays and drones as we go to give the slowpokes a clear visual.*>

<*You're so kind,*> Shoshin commented as the AM-4s touched down on the platform.

With her mechs all present, Rika divvied out the rest of the targets.

<*Yig and Cole, you two take the storage facility on the right. Shoshin and Goob, you have the one on the left. The Van and I will stay in reserve.*>

<*Need your beauty rest, Van?*> Goob asked with a laugh as he and Shoshin moved to the left side of the platform, lining up with a catwalk below.

The K1R's low chuckle rumbled in their minds. <*Not likely to get any, with you blundering around out there. Kelly and I already have a bet going, on how long it'll take for you to call me in.*>

<*Screw you, Van,*> Goob shot back.

<*Relax, people,*> Rika said in her most soothing voice. <*We just have to stop a few Niets from blowing the station with some*

antimatter. This is a cakewalk.>

<Great,> Niki groaned. *<Now you've gone and done it.>*

<Hey,> Kelly piped up from a catwalk her team had climbed to. *<Fred's team* ***did*** *actually lay eyes on our friendly neighborhood Niets, right? I mean…shouldn't the bad guys be here already?>*

Rika had been wondering the same thing. There were plenty of places to hide in the massive space, but if the enemy was after the antimatter, there were only so many routes they could take, most of them out in the open.

She re-checked the most expedient routes to the facility from where Fred had encountered the Niets, and could only conclude that Kelly was right: they should have seen some sign of them by now.

<Stay sharp, people. Either they know we're here and they're waiting for…something—>

<Or they have another goal,> Niki interjected.

Rika reviewed the station's layout, looking for some other possible objective—either escape or destruction—but determined that, unless the Nietzscheans planned to dive out of an airlock, there wasn't any other reason for the enemy to come down to engineering.

<Contacts!> Kelly announced, and Rika breathed a sigh of relief—an unexpected reaction for running into a group of Nietzscheans who were planning to destroy a station.

<Shit! Got some here too,> Goob added.

The Van snorted. *<Do you need rescuing yet?>*

<Fuck!> Goob swore. *<There's at least thirty of them, they're spread all over, hiding behind D2 tanks.>*

Rika glanced over her shoulder at where she knew the stealthed K1R to be standing. *<Better go help him. Do your shield thing.>*

<Easy,> The Van grunted.

By the time the mech was on his way to aid Goob, Shoshin and Cole were engaged as well. Rika watched her mechs' feeds, ready to move to a team's aid, but each group's progress was inexorable, and she was confident that they'd reach the antimatter storage facilities before the Niets.

<*Any sign of the colonel?*> she asked her team a few minutes later.

<*Sure, she's back where we dropped down, sipping a cold one,*> Kelly replied with a laugh.

<*The* ***enemy*** *colonel, wiseass,*> Niki shot back.

<*We've secured the entrance to our storage room,*> Goob reported. <*No sign of the coward yet.*>

<*No sign here, either,*> Kelly replied. <*Just one more squad to dig out, and we'll have our target secure.*>

<*Slowpokes,*> Shoshin said a few seconds later. <*Our antimatter is secure.*>

<*We can see your feeds,*> Fiona laughed in response. <*You made it, but you're pinned down. Need a hand?*>

Rika was about to leave the platform to help Shoshin's team when Niki flashed an updated log entry on her HUD.

Shit.

<*Fiona, peel off and get Shoshin and Cole an exit. I think I know where the colonel is.*>

<*You going alone?*> The Van asked.

<*Just recon,*> Rika assured him. <*Turns out that there might be a ship in one of the docking bays two decks below this place.*>

Kelly snorted. <*Dude's the ultimate douche. Sends his troops to secure antimatter to blow the station while he buggers off.*>

<*Be a good cover if he can time it right,*> Cole allowed.

<*Whose side are you on?*> Kelly retorted.

Rika shook her head as she turned and loped across the platform. <*Everyone, stay on your objectives.*> She reached out to Chase on the command net. <*We're just a few minutes from locking down all the antimatter. How are things up there?*>

<Our people are just about off the station,> he replied. *<We've shoved the Niets into escape pods, and the few civvies that were left on the station have already blasted off. Heather's tracking them so we can scoop up any strays later on.>*

Rika nodded absently as she sent a pair of drones down the passageway at the end of the platform. *<Just make sure she keeps the* Fury Lance *nearby. If this Niet colonel does have a way off-station, I want her ready to scoop him up, too.>*

<All the scooping. Got it.>

Rika smiled to herself as she rushed down the corridor in the wake of her drones, reaching a lift that would take her down the two levels.

She sent a drone in to activate the conveyance, and lobbed a grenade inside before the doors closed. She set the drone to detonate the explosive the moment the doors opened on the lower level. No staircase provided an alternate route down, but there was an access shaft with a ladder a few meters away.

As the lift descended, Rika pulled a panel off the shaft and jumped inside, certain that the Niets would not have had time to secure it against her advance.

She was halfway down to the lower level when it turned out that she was only half right.

A soldier eased into view below her and fired up at Rika as she fell. She didn't have a good angle with either of her rifles, so she weathered the barrage, rounds chipping away at her armor, until her three-clawed feet were in range, and she clamped one on the Niet's head.

Her momentum pulled the soldier into the shaft and finally provided Rika with a good firing angle for her GNR. A trio of kinetic rounds burst from the weapon's muzzle and tore the enemy's shoulder off.

The Niet screamed as he fell, and Rika sent a few more rounds his way to make sure he wouldn't come back up.

She caught the edge of the opening onto the lower deck and was pulling herself up into the corridor when the lift doors opened and the grenade exploded. She saw a body fly past, and used the distraction to leap out and fall prone in the passageway, firing with her AC9CR rifle at a stunned-looking enemy soldier a few meters ahead.

Another Nietzschean was on her left, clearly dead, and Rika turned away, sending out a fresh pair of drones to scout ahead as she rose.

The drones barely stayed ahead of her as she loped down the hundred meters of twisting passages, no additional enemies in evidence until she caught sight of the bay.

She slowed her pace, triggering her armor to shed heat and resume full stealth before she approached. Her drones ranged closer and gave her a view of two soldiers standing next to the ramp while the colonel paced back and forth in front of it.

<*Well, he's clearly waiting for something,*> Niki commented as the colonel stopped and shook his head, cursing before he resumed wearing a groove in the deck.

<*Color me curious,*> Rika replied as she quietly walked into the bay, taking care to move silently across the grated deck. <*Think he's waiting for a person, or intel?*>

<*Let me consult my crystal ball.*>

<*Funny.*>

<*Get close and land some nano on him, then we'll find out.*>

Rika was surprised at Niki's suggestion. <*You're going to breach his mind?*>

<*No, I'm not a monster, Rika. I'm just going to tap his Link. Why would you think I'd do that?*>

<*Well…*> She paused, wondering why she had in fact leapt to that conclusion. <*You did suggest blowing this station with all hands.*>

<*Not with all hands!*> Niki almost shouted the denial. <*We would have given them warning and let them hit evac pods.*>

<*Oh!*> Rika felt herself redden. <*I guess that makes sense. Not sure why I assumed differently.*>

The AI laughed. <*I wonder if it has something to do with the fact that you've only slept a handful of hours in the past week.*>

<*I suppose that could be a contributing factor.*>

Rika crept up to the pacing colonel, stopping just a meter from the point where he turned, and reached out, flicking a small blob of infiltration nano onto his back during his next passage.

<*OK, locating his antenna…standard placement,*> Niki said as she got to work. <*Oh! New crypto algorithms. The Niets are finally getting wise.*>

<*About time,*> Rika muttered. <*Though I guess we've been advancing at the speed of information. They only know we're coming days before we arrive in most cases.*>

<*If that. However, they're still using the same root keys, from the looks of it. All I have to do is—*>

The colonel spun, his eyes searching the bay, and Rika froze—though she knew there was no way he could see her. A second later, something hit her in the back, and she swore, realizing she'd been hit by a gel bomb, the sticky substance ruining her stealth.

<*Buy me another minute,*> Niki said.

"Dammit. How'd you spot me?" Rika asked the colonel, noting that both the soldiers had raised their rifles, though curiously hadn't yet fired.

I wonder if they know I'll drop them before they get a second round off.

"Not about to share that with a mech," the colonel said. "I take it you're not my courier."

<*Drone fired the blob,*> Niki supplied. <*No idea how it saw us.*>

The idea that the Niets might have figured out a way to outsmart ISF stealth tech set Rika's nerves on edge, but only solidified her desire to take the colonel alive so she could learn how he'd managed it.

"Well, I have a message for you, does that count?" she asked him.

"Not really, no," the Nietzschean replied. "You're an SMI, from what I can see of you. Not Rika herself, by any chance, are you?"

Something in his voice told her that she'd best keep her cards close to her chest, and she shook her head. "No such luck—well, luck for you, I suppose. She might just kill you. I have orders to capture."

"You're going to find that a bit hard," the man said, and Rika found herself wondering what reason he had for such a high level of confidence.

She decided to remove his options, and two bursts fired from her GNR, tearing the two guards' arms off, sending the soldiers to the deck while their weapons spun away.

The colonel appeared nonplussed. "Brutal, just like all your kind."

She didn't rise to the bait, instead nodding at his sidearm. "Your weapon. Drop it."

The Nietzschean shrugged and pulled his weapon free, tossing it away.

<*Progress?*> Rika asked Niki.

<*Yes, just about—oh shit!*>

Alerts flared on Rika's HUD, indicating security breaches all across her armor. Her right leg suddenly gave out, and she fell to a knee, her body beginning to spasm.

<*The gel was loaded with nano,*> Niki said lamely. <*And our reserves are low…dammit.*>

Rika knew that she was about to be out of options, and triggered a rapid blow-off of her armor in an attempt to keep more nano from breaching her systems. At the same time, Niki triggered a defensive surface charge that electrified Rika's skin.

Only half her armor fell off, and though the measure helped, the control systems in her legs still weren't responding. She tried to bring her GNR around to fire on the colonel, but her arm wouldn't respond, either.

"Always nice to watch a mech in its dying throes," the Nietzschean said as he walked over to one of his soldiers' rifles and picked it up.

Rika managed to gain enough control of her gun arm to bring her GNR around, but there was no strength in her limb, and the enemy colonel took two quick strides forward and easily kicked it aside.

He brought his own weapon to bear, aiming it at her neck. "Might be something useful in your head."

<Niki! Options!>

<Fifteen seconds and I'll have him breached. Just don't die.>

Rika was about to offer her surrender to buy time, when the colonel's head disappeared.

"Nothing useful in yours." The Van's deep rumble came from behind Rika.

"Shit, Van!" she swore, collapsing to the deck. "What the hell?"

"You're welcome, Colonel?" the K1R asked.

Rika wanted to rail against the mech, but he knew he'd done the right thing. It was she who had stupidly trusted her tech too much, putting herself in needless danger.

"Sorry, Van," Rika said as she fell back to the deck. "Any chance you have an armor rack tucked somewhere in all that gear?"

RETREAT

STELLAR DATE: 05.18.8950 (Adjusted Years)
LOCATION: NMS *Kraska*, 45 AU from Luxom
REGION: Genevia System, New Genevian Alliance

Admiral Hammond's lips drew into a thin line as he reviewed the latest report from within the Genevia System. Most of it was what he expected: defeats.

He'd held out hope that Colonel Florin's mission on Lisbon Station would have met with success, but unfortunately, it had not.

For the time being, the plans were lost to him.

An overwhelming urge to smash something came over Hammond, but he tamped it down, knowing that at least now, the Nietzschean Empire would have strong leadership, not Constantine's grasping ambitions.

With nothing left to fight for in Genevia—or nothing that they could secure—the admiral knew that it was time to return to the Nietzschea System.

The news of the defeat at Genevia would not go over well with the High Council, but it would be nothing compared to how they'd received the news of the emperor's death. Constantine had ruled for over thirty years and had no heirs, a deliberate decision on his part intended to keep entitled children from assassinating him.

With no clear succession, control of the empire would go to whoever made the strongest claim. Though Hammond had long been at Constantine's side, he was not the highest-ranking officer in the Nietzschean space force. There were several admirals with more seniority than he, topmost of which was Admiral Yara.

She would make an immediate play for control of the

empire. That would likely involve the immediate death or arrest—on some trumped-up charge—of Lord Poulos, leader of the High Council.

"It's going to be a civil war if we're not careful," he mused, rising from his desk and turning to face the window, which showed a view he *would* have seen, should the window have been real, and were he not deep within the bowels of the *Kraska*.

The ship was over fifty AU from the Genevian star, the brightest point of light in the display. Nestled close around that ball of fusing hydrogen lay the fleet that had utterly defeated his forces and now put all of Nietzschea in peril.

The Marauders.

But it was not just *their* ships. The vaunted ISF fleet was present as well, come to the mercenaries' aid. Every one of those ships was equipped with stasis shields that were impenetrable when pitted against standard weaponry. Had the *Pinnacle*'s main weapon been in place, it would have been able to destroy the enemy, but even so, just one stasis-killer wasn't enough to defeat an entire fleet.

And that was the real problem. Hammond understood it well, but he was certain that the power-hungry lords and admirals back in Nietzschea would not. They would not easily be convinced of the magnitude of the threat.

Key to that was the fact that Colonel Rika and her Marauders had not eased their way through the former Genevian Alliance, liberating key systems and building up support; no, they'd lanced straight through the systems of Old Genevia and attacked the heart of their former nation.

Because of that, Hammond believed that Rika would not slow to engage Nietzschean occupiers in neighboring systems.

They're going to drive straight for the core of the Empire. Rika's next stop will be the Nietzschea System itself.

It felt absurd, thinking those words. A month ago, he would have laughed, should anyone have told him that.

What he needed was time. Time to convince the other admirals that the Marauders were an existential threat, and that the war with Genevia was back on.

<*Sir?*> The tired voice of Hammond's chief aide came into his mind.

<*What is it, Major Fennel?*>

<*There is a man named Doctor Xa here to see you.*>

The name sparked immediate recognition, and Hammond initiated a privacy field in his office.

<*Send him in.*>

The door opened, and a slim, unassuming man stepped in. He moved with a casual grace, his face calm, almost serene—completely out of character for a civilian doctor on a warship fleeing after a defeat.

But Hammond knew that this was no simple doctor he faced.

"I didn't know you had made it aboard, Xa," he said by way of greeting, gesturing to the chair across from his desk, while he returned to his own seat.

"I almost didn't," the man replied as he sat. "I got off Belgium and onto one of the corvettes. The ship's captain wanted to engage the Marauders, but I convinced her otherwise. My life is not to be so cheaply squandered."

The admiral nodded. "I understand your sentiment."

"So the emperor is dead." Xa's voice contained no emotion as he uttered the words. "And you are returning to Nietzschea to attempt to keep the fools there focused on the real enemy, I assume?"

Hammond let out a weary sigh. "That is my primary goal, though I am going to dispatch couriers with orders for a few nearby systems."

"Oh?" the doctor asked. "What are you going to have them

do?"

The admiral's eyes narrowed. "Scorched earth."

"You want to slow the Marauders down."

"Yes. We'll create humanitarian crises in neighboring systems, split Colonel Rika's focus, and force her to move to protect other systems before we do the same there. I need to buy us time to prepare for her assault against Nietzschea."

The doctor shook his head. "What will that do? When they show up—and they *will* come—no fleet will be able to stand up to their stasis ships. What you're facing now is a steady retreat toward a final stand in some backwater system on the far edge of the empire."

Hammond's calm veneer slipped away and a sneer formed on his lips. "Oh? Well what would you have me do, great Chief of Spies? Please, tell me this brilliant strategy you have."

"You need to sue for peace," Xa said.

The admiral barked a laugh. "Maybe that's why we lost and the emperor died."

"What is?"

"Because you're a fool!" Hammond roared. "If you think that Colonel Rika and her mechs are going to stop before they raze Nietzschea to the ground, then you're an idiot. You know how Psych has profiled her. She won't stop for peace negotiations—and why should she? It'll take her a few years to wipe us out, but like you said, the empire's days are numbered."

"You are correct. *Rika* is the enemy's galvanizing force. Undertake your scorched earth strategy, Admiral. Nothing so extreme that it will galvanize the Genevians against us, just enough to weaken nearby systems to the point where the Marauders will have to provide aid and protection."

The other man paused, and Hammond raised his hand, twirling his finger in a circle. "Carry on, spy."

"Then I cut the head off the snake."

"You think you can kill Rika?"

Xa nodded. "She's just a woman—not even that, less than *half* a woman. A machine with another machine embedded in her mind. Even more, she's young, foolish. She may be a formidable opponent on the field of battle, but once she's forced to stop moving, pressed to consolidate her power, she will be playing my game. The game of politics."

"You think you can get close to her?"

"Yes. Many of our assets are still in place…. I'll rebuild the network in Genevia and leverage it to gain access to the Marauder colonel. She's not defenseless, so I'll need time to assess her weaknesses. But your activities will distract her, tire her, wear her down. And then I'll strike."

"And then, with her dead, the Genevians will keep their focus within their own borders." Hammond lifted a hand to his chin, running a finger along his jawline. "Then we extend an olive branch to her successor."

"Not to *them,*" Xa corrected. "Rika is an agent of the Alliance's field marshal. We plead our case to Tangel. If reports are to be believed, she is fighting a war across half the Orion Arm of the galaxy. Having one less front to fight will not displease her."

Hammond knew the devil would be in the details, but the spy's plan had merit. At the very least, it would buy more time to mount some sort of defense against the enemy.

"And what's more," Xa continued in a low voice as he leant forward, "I can get agents aboard the *Pinnacle* and access its plans. That way, we'll be able to halt their stasis ships, should our hope of a truce fail. What say you?"

The Nietzschean admiral rose and extended his hand, which Xa clasped in his own a moment later.

"I'd say, Doctor Xa, that we have a plan. Time to execute it."

"And Colonel Rika."

RECUPERATING

STELLAR DATE: 05.18.8950 (Adjusted Years)
LOCATION: *Fury Lance*, en route to Belgium
REGION: Genevia System, New Genevian Alliance

Rika was first at the table—a rarity, given the number of demands on her time. However, she'd made a point of shunting as much work as possible into tomorrow's queue to make time for this event.

The evening was to be a night for celebration with her commanders. So far as they knew, the last pockets of Nietzschean resistance had been neutralized; the Genevia System was well and truly theirs.

"Now the real work begins," Rika said, her rueful laugh echoing off the wood-paneled walls of the officer's dining room.

<*Well, you've been avoiding it long enough. Time to dig in.*> Niki's tone was only moderately scolding.

"I haven't been avoiding anything. We had to dig out the Niets and ensure that the system doesn't devolve into chaos. That's more important than most of the other nonsense that's landing in my lap."

<*Nonsense such as sorting out how people are going to eat, what to do with merchant ships entering the system, fuel supplies, rearmament, prisoners of war…?*>

Rika's lips drew into a thin line. "Yeah, I get that all of that is important, it just wasn't as important as the final battles were. But starting tomorrow, those items will get all my focus."

"I hope not *all* your focus," a voice said, and Rika looked up from the table to see Chase striding through the room's doorway.

"I mean my work focus," she retorted while rising. "You know there's always time for us focus."

A soft laugh rumbled in his throat as he approached with open arms. Rika rose and met his embrace.

Both of the mechs were wearing their more natural limbs—Rika out of necessity, with her combat limbs in repair—and their bodies from the neck down were a matte grey, the default configuration of the ISF Mark X FlowArmor skin that was their epidermis.

Though it was nice to not always be sheathed in armor and hard edges, Rika still felt naked when her body appeared almost like a normal human's. Chase seemed more at ease in his natural limbs, but then, he had only been a mech for a year. Rika had spent over a decade with her body more machine than woman, so looking like a squishie still felt foreign to her—as though it were the disguise.

"Good," Chase said as he settled into the seat at Rika's right side. "Because all shooting and no sex makes Chase a grumpy guy."

"I don't see why that has to be an either/or scenario," she replied. "Though I suppose they're difficult to do simultaneously."

"I'm willing to try anything at least once."

"A man after my own heart," Sergeant Major Barne said as he strode into the dining room with Captain Leslie at his side.

Barne and Leslie had been with Rika almost as long as Chase. They were part of the first team she'd been assigned to in the Marauders, a spec-ops group known as 'Basilisk'.

There were only two people in the world who had been a part of Rika's life longer: Kelly—who was likely in the enlisted mess, engaged in a drinking game of some sort—and Major Silva, who entered the room right on Leslie and Barne's heels.

After being mechanized during the first war between

Genevia and Nietzschea, Rika had found herself assigned to a scout mech team that went by the name of Hammerfall. Silva had been the leader of that team, and the woman who had helped Rika deal with the fact that she'd been conscripted and chopped up by her own people, turned into a machine to fight a war they'd ultimately lost.

When the war had ended, and the Genevian Armed Forces surrendered, Rika and Silva had lost track of one another, but a year ago, they'd been reunited when Team Basilisk rescued Silva's daughter and overthrew a tyrant who was using mechs to build an army.

Mechs who were now the bulk of Rika's battalion.

"So, what's on the menu?" Barne asked as he settled into a seat on the far side of Chase. "And has this room always been on the *Lance?* Why don't we eat here more often?"

"Because we want it to stay nice," Leslie chided. "If we ate here on a regular basis, you'd probably carve your initials into the table."

Barne snorted. "Who says I haven't already?"

"You carve up my table, and we're gonna have a problem, Barne," Captain Heather said as she walked into the room followed by Captains Scarcliff, Penny, Klen, and Travis.

"Gonna have to remember not to invite you to the captain's table on the *Republic,*" Travis added.

"Least you have a nice captain's table," Klen sulked. "The *Asora* just has a plas slab."

"Do you want a nicer table?" Rika asked. "I imagine we could get you one."

Klen shrugged. "Sure, would be nice, I guess, though there's rarely more than a dozen of us on the ship, and we eat in the main mess."

"Then what are you complaining about?" Barne asked.

"I guess I get the urge to grouse about pretty much everything from being close to you, Master Sergeant."

Barne opened his mouth to respond, but then the last diner entered the room.

"Sorry I'm late," Colonel Borden said as he settled into the seat at the far end of the table. "Debriefing took a bit longer than I'd expected."

"ISF. Late as always," Barne said, laughing as he shook his head.

Borden shrugged, used to Barne's needling at this point. "I could always let Admiral Carson know he's not needed here anymore. I imagine there's a battle he could join elsewhere."

"OK, folks," Rika held up a hand, knowing that the group would happily needle one another for hours, given the opportunity. "Let's see if we can have a nice, celebratory dinner without starting some new inter-force competition."

"Because the ISF would win," Borden added.

"You know..." Heather mused. "I wonder if we should have some sort of game when we get back to Belgium. A celebration of the Nietzschean defeat."

"That's a really good idea." Chase nodded as a servitor set a glass of wine in front of him. "We should mark the occasion. It would be good for both civilian and military morale."

The others nodded in agreement, and a toothy grin found its way onto Borden's face. "Tell me, then. Are your mechs any good at football?"

"What kind of football?" Barne asked. "There must be a thousand games that involve kicking a ball."

Borden's grin faded into a look of mock-shock. "*The* football. The first one."

<I think the 'first one' was played in China over twelve thousand years ago,> Niki supplied. *<Pretty sure that's not what you're referring to, Colonel.>*

"Well, no. By 'first one', I mean the version that gets called 'soccer'. It was *the* sport back when we left Sol."

<*Ah, Terran soccer.*> Niki displayed rules and basic information in a holodisplay above the table. <*There are a few similar games played in this region of space.*>

"Kick a ball on a field into a net?" Barne read. "Can't touch the ball with your hands.... Seems simple enough."

The ISF colonel's brows knit. "Nothing simple about it—as your mechs will soon find out."

"Do you really think that your Marines can compete against Marauders?" Barne scoffed.

Rika wondered how such a contest would play out. The Marauders could easily field a team consisting only of mechs, formidable opponents to be sure. However, the ISF Marines were hardly stock human—though they looked it on the outside.

"I like the idea." She made the proclamation with a note of finality in her voice. "We'll do it in five days. That'll give us enough time to set up a venue and get the system excited for the contest."

"You sure?" Travis asked. "There's a lot to do—some people may think we're being frivolous."

"Mechs? Frivolous?" Leslie snorted a laugh. "It would be good for your image if you showed a fun side. Humanize you more in the eyes of the people."

"Irony, your name is Leslie," Chase said, shaking his head as he laughed.

Rika took his meaning without trouble. Most of the mechs at the table had their natural-looking limbs attached, and Borden appeared to be entirely normal—albeit a very *large* normal. Leslie, on the other hand, was still sporting the cat-like appearance that she'd adopted in the Peloponnese System over a year ago. Jet black skin, a tail, long ears, and pupils that narrowed to vertical slits.

Topping it off, she'd added retractable claws on her hands and feet at some point. Rika had joined in a pool with a few other Marauders as to when she'd add fangs to the mix.

"You trying to make a point? I don't *want* to be humanized." Her tail whipped around Barne and tapped Chase in the back of the head. "This is more 'me' than stock human ever was."

"A sentiment most of us share," Rika replied, earning a wave of nods from around the table.

Though most mechs had been turned into half-machine warriors against their will, they all had been given the opportunity to become flesh and blood humans again—and they'd all declined. In fact, Vargo Klen, Chase, and Barne had all volunteered to become mechs, the change giving them a stronger sense of belonging in Rika's Marauders.

Borden shrugged. "The only strange thing about you is that you choose to look less natural than you have to. Though I have to admit that I like the idea of a configurable buildout. A few of my Marines have expressed interest in trying out swappable limbs like you lot use."

"Mechanized Marines." Klen nodded in approval. "They'd kick even more ass."

"*All* the asses would be kicked," Barne said.

As the group spoke, the servitors had set everyone's preferred drinks in front of them, and Rika held up her glass of bubbly white wine. "A toast. To the Marauders and the ISF, and to our future as the Genevian Armed Forces."

"To Rika," Barne said on the heels of her statement. "Without her, we would not be here."

"To Rika!" the others echoed, and then drank from their glasses.

With a gracious smile, she joined them, taking a long drought.

"I just have one suggestion," Heather said as she set her glass back down. "Can we *not* be the Genevian Armed Forces?

Being in the 'GAF' doesn't exactly have a lot of happy memories for me. I'd hate to cringe every time I hear my military's name."

"Do you have any suggestions?" Rika asked.

"What about the New Genevian Military?" Barne suggested.

Leslie cocked an eyebrow. "Are we officially going with 'New Genevia'?"

"It's what the Blue Ridge and Iberian systems are already calling themselves," Barne replied. "Seems like it would be easy to go along with that."

"I'm not against it." Rika liked the fact that it was still clearly Genevia, but different from the old nation at the same time—a distinction she felt was necessary for her mechs.

"Could go with NGSF," Heather suggested. " 'Space Force' instead of 'Military'."

"Not sure how the ground pounders would feel about that," Chase said.

"My Marines are all space force," Colonel Borden said. "None of them are bothered by it."

"Yeah, but the ISF has always had a *strong* space force," Barne countered. "The GAF's used to suck ass."

"You don't say?" Borden drawled. "Not like I haven't been with you Marauders for the past year. I've heard all the stories."

"Year's not long enough for *all* the stories," Heather muttered. "But I still say we go with 'NGSF'."

Barne barked a laugh. "So many stories. 'NGSF' works for me as well."

"Well, I'll keep those in mind," Rika said. "I'll run them past the other company commanders when we meet back up at Belgium. Tremon, too."

Those gathered around the table nodded, and after a moment of silence, Borden spoke up.

"So, do you think you can really get a football team together in five days? Seriously now, don't get an old man's hopes up."

THE REFUGE

STELLAR DATE: 05.18.8950 (Adjusted Years)
LOCATION: The Refuge, Faneuil
REGION: Genevia System, New Genevian Alliance

Oda stood at the edge of The Refuge's Central Park, watching a group of children playing on the grass, tossing a ball back and forth without a care given for the troubles that lay beyond the stone ceiling high above.

Their antics served to remind him of the purpose of the secret facility tucked deep inside Faneuil: the preservation of true Genevian society. The Genevia that lay outside the facility was twisted and worn from the long occupation by the Nietzscheans.

No clearer evidence was needed than the fact that mechs were in leadership positions.

The things were abominations, criminals whose minds were warped by Discipline, the system that had controlled them and kept them from turning on their own during the war. A system they no longer possessed.

Colonel Rika had informed him that the ISF—a military born from an ancient colony ship, the *Intrepid*—had upgraded the mechs, permanently freeing them from the Discipline system. She had spoken of that 'upgrade' as though it was a wonderful advancement, a great liberation.

To him, it had spelled terror.

And now Rika was in a position to take control of the Genevia System, and possibly all of the Genevian Alliance.

A colonel, and a mech.

Not only that, but she was practically a child, a mere thirty years of age.

Oda had hoped that President Kalvin, or Tremon, as he

called himself now, would see sense and take the reins. But the former president hadn't made a move to re-establish his position. It seemed as though he was content to operate as Rika's advisor, guiding her.

The fact that Tremon would make himself subservient to a mech only further demonstrated how broken everything was outside of The Refuge.

I have to move fast, or things are going to get far worse before they get better.

Though Oda's network of spies had taken losses during the battle to regain control of the Genevia System, he still had assets in the field, people he could use to ensure that Genevia was never ruled by a mech—or anyone else other than him, for that matter.

Right on schedule, a figure strolled onto the park's cool lawn, skirting the children as he moved toward Oda.

A rare smile graced Oda's lips. "Time to put old plans in motion."

THE OLD PRESIDENT

STELLAR DATE: 05.20.8950 (Adjusted Years)
LOCATION: *Fury Lance*, Belgium
REGION: Genevia System, New Genevian Alliance

The *Fury Lance* hadn't even settled into its high orbit around Belgium before Chief Ona turned and gave Rika an understanding look.

"STC has just informed us that a shuttle is departing from the Mount Genevia Spaceport. They're requesting clearance to route it to us."

Rika knew that the shuttle's origination, and Space Traffic Control's forwarding of the request, could mean only one thing.

She nodded to Captain Heather, and the SMI-4 addressed Ona. "Grant them permission. Docking bay 14."

"Aye, ma'am." The LHO mech's four limbs danced across her console, and she nodded a moment later. "Berth confirmed."

Heather gave Rika a knowing look. "He's not going to be happy that you went on the mission."

"Yeah, well, he's not the boss of me." She was trying to be funny, but realized her comment just came off as whiny. "Stars. I take that back. But he's still not in charge."

"Doesn't mean he doesn't have a point."

The captain's expression was unreadable, but the fact she'd given voice to the words was enough. Even so, it wasn't a conversation Rika wanted to have in earshot of the crew.

<*Well, unless he wants to be president again, he can't order me around,*> she addressed Heather privately. <*Core, even if he **were** the president, I'm outside his chain of command.*>

<*Even taking politics out of it, Rika, you still need to remember*

that you're the battalion's CO,> Heather countered. *<You're not a frontline soldier anymore.>*

Rika gave the captain a level stare that brooked no argument. *<I'll always be a frontline soldier. Even if Kelly and Jenisa were to have their way and see me made queen, I'd be a warrior queen.>*

<Well, I recommend you promote yourself before that,> Heather said, her lips twisting into a wry smile. *<Can't have a queen who is only a colonel.>*

<Technically, we're all still Marauders. We have contracts,> Rika replied. *<General Julia would need to promote me.>*

<Not if we become the NGSF,> Heather said with a wink.

<Yeah,> Rika nodded as she walked toward the bridge's exit. *<That's another thing I need to do—figure out how to legally separate from the Marauders and not have to turn everything over to General Julia.>*

<Well, figure it out soon, because right now, the mechs feel like they're in limbo. Everyone hates limbo.>

<It's near the top of my list,> Rika assured her. *<You done giving me a hard time? I need a few minutes to recover before Tremon starts in on me.>*

The *Fury Lance*'s captain barked a laugh. *<Yeah, I'm good. And I'm sorry…I didn't mean to. We'll get all this sorted soon enough.>*

<Yeah.>

Rika gave the noncommittal response from out in the corridor that led to the administrative area aft of the bridge. The sounds of people hard at work, managing the ship and the Marauder fleet at large, came to her, the hum of activity a familiar comfort.

Though the *Fury Lance* had been Rika's flagship for over a year, it had never really felt properly lived in. The reason for that was simple: the four-kilometer-long vessel could house thousands, but the typical Marauder complement was just a few hundred.

But now that her ship was effectively the center of government for the re-emerging alliance, everyone who wanted a voice in the New Genevian government had found their way aboard, inserting themselves into the decision-making process.

The conversations in the administration area grew muted as she walked through the atrium, those gathered around holotanks and desks glancing her way and straightening as she passed. Some of them were mechs, a few more were human Marauders, others were Genevians who were trying to secure resources for their corners of the system.

No, that's not fair, she thought. *A lot of them have come forward to help. Don't let the few bad apples ruin the bunch.*

By some miracle, no one stopped her with an emergency that required her attention, and after passing through the administrative area, she walked in silence through the ship, nodding in greeting to any crew she passed, her thoughts churning over the work that lay ahead of her.

The problem she grappled with was that she couldn't decide what to do next. Genevia was the fourth system her Marauders had liberated; in all the others, she'd struck hard and fast, then moved on in just a few weeks. Already, she'd been in the Genevia System longer than any other since….

<Shit, Niki. Last time I was in a system for this long, I was working in Hal's Hell in Parsons.>

<Best get used to this one. We'll be here a bit longer.>

<Think that's what's under my skin?> Rika asked.

<What? That you have ants in your pants?>

A shudder rippled through Rika at the thought. Being a mech, she didn't wear pants—which meant that any ants would be crawling around in her armor. That had happened before, and it made for a nasty cleanup job.

<I'd like to remain ant-free, thank you.>

<You know what I mean,> Niki chided. *<You need to reorient your mindset. Accept the fact that you're going to be in the Genevia System for the foreseeable future.>*

<I need a better plan than 'the foreseeable future',> Rika countered, shaking her head in frustration as she stepped onto the lift that would take her down to Bay 14.

<Well, this would go a lot faster if the system had a clear and absolute leader,> Niki prompted.

Rika didn't respond to the AI's statement, remaining silent the rest of the way to the bay.

A week ago, in the heat of the battle, she'd laughed along when her Marauders had joked about her being crowned queen. Though she suspected Kelly and Jenisa were sincere, she'd believed that everyone else had been kidding.

She'd been wrong.

<We should work to find a clear leader, then,> Rika said as she reached Bay 14, looking out through the grav shield to see the shuttle on approach. *<My primary goal is to get this fleet ready to move on to Nietzschea. Maybe even by jump gate, if the ISF will supply us with the mirrors for our ships.>*

<That's going to take a while and you know it. The Niets are going to have tens of thousands of ships at their capital—we'll need to jump in with an overwhelming force. Heck, we should expect the civilians to join in against us.>

Rika wasn't so sure about that. Many of the Nietzschean merchant ships that had entered the Genevia System in the past week had readily accepted the system's change in management.

That was one benefit of the enemy's master morality. They recognized when there was a new master.

Even so, she'd debated this matter with Niki several times, and would be having the same conversation with Tremon in a few minutes. She wasn't looking forward to seeing how many times she could have the debate in a day.

The fact that it was even a debate to begin with was what bothered Rika the most. In battle, her mechs followed orders without hesitation. Her ships were where she needed them, when she needed them. There was no discussion.

But when it came to rebuilding the nation, everyone wanted to have their say.

I suppose that's fair, to a degree, she allowed.

Entering Bay 14, she calmed her mind, preparing for that and whatever else Tremon would level at her. The fact that he hadn't reached out over the Link during his approach was enough to convince her that it wasn't going to be fun. The former president always liked to have important conversations face-to-face.

A minute later, the shuttle was on the docking cradle. Before the ramp had lifted from the deck, the airlock was cycling open, revealing Tremon looking even more dour than usual.

Rika scolded herself for the uncharitable thought. The former president of Genevia carried a heavy weight on his shoulders, blaming himself for the defeat that the alliance had suffered at the hands of the Nietzscheans.

The Marauders under Rika's command had forgiven him for his part in the war that saw the end of Old Genevia. No one wanted to dwell on past mistakes and assign blame—there was enough to go around.

It seemed to take forever, but the ramp finally rose within a half meter of the airlock, and Tremon leapt down onto it; his personal guard, Yakob, following after a moment later. When they reached the bottom, Rika extended her hand.

"It's good to see you, Tremon."

"And you, Colonel Rika," he replied, his calm voice a stark contrast to the frustration visible on his face. "I'm glad you had your fun shooting Niets. Things have been a bit more trying back here."

"More trying than Niets with antimatter bombs?" she asked, glancing at Yakob and giving him a nod. "I suspect nothing so dire has happened in my absence—not that came to my attention, at least."

She hadn't shared the details of the encounter with the Nietzschean colonel with anyone other than her inner circle, for now wanting to ensure that rumors of an ability to see stealthed mechs didn't spread. So far as Tremon knew, the antimatter had been the worst of it.

Tremon's lips twisted and he sighed, nodding in agreement. "Perhaps nothing so immediately urgent as that, but trust me, it is a serious matter."

Rika gestured to the bay's interior doors. "There's a briefing room down the passage. Let's talk there."

The former president seemed to suddenly realize that there were others in the bay, technicians moving to service the shuttle, and a few pilots playing a game of snark atop a nearby crate.

"Yes, yes, of course," he grunted and followed Rika as she led the way out the bay and into the corridor.

"And here I thought you'd come up here to chide me for taking part in the assault on Lisbon," she said once they were out of the bay.

"I would," Tremon ground out the words, "if I thought it would do any good."

"Me being in the field is the very definition of good," Rika countered.

"For you, maybe. Look, Rika, I don't have the energy to have that debate right now. You lead from the front. I get that—it drives me nuts, but by the same token, you've met with incredible success, so I'm not going to contest your methods."

She didn't bother to hide her surprise at his words and nodded appreciatively. "OK…I suppose we can just leave that be for now."

"Good," he replied, following her into the briefing room.

Yakob peered inside, seemed satisfied that no assassins were going to jump out from under the table within, and then took up a position in the hall.

"So what's this about?" Rika asked as the door slid shut.

"Oda." Tremon said the name with clear distaste. "He's prepared an official proclamation that since The Refuge housed the 'Government in Exile', and he is the leader there, he is the de facto president of Genevia. And that Faneuil should be the capital."

Rika gasped. "What?"

She was more than happy for someone else to take the reins of power—just so long as that someone wasn't Oda.

Not only that, but The Refuge's position was far from ideal. The secret facility lay within a dwarf planet named Faneuil in the far reaches of the Genevia System. It was there that a group of rebels—though ones with little interest in fomenting an actual rebellion—had resided since the fall of Genevia.

Over the years, they'd become complacent, happy to live in their hidden world, doing little to forward the cause they purported to support.

Even when Rika came to them with the means to defeat the Nietzscheans and kill their emperor, Oda and his people had refused to help, instead attempting to actively obstruct the Marauders' operations.

"Faneuil. Really?"

"He's calling for it to be the location of the government until Belgium can be 'properly secured'," Tremon clarified.

Rika snorted. "Which is to say that he's lived in his hidey hole for so long, he's afraid to come out. But that doesn't explain why I hadn't heard anything about this proclamation."

"He's sent the message out to a number of his contacts, pre-seeding it around the system so it can transmit simultaneously on the disparate worlds. I got wind of it because I still have a few friends here who prefer me to Oda."

"I should hope that everyone would prefer you to Oda," Rika muttered. "OK, what do we do?"

Tremon leant back against the table, placing his hands on the edge. His dark eyes locked on hers. "You know what we have to do."

"Seriously?" she asked. "That's our only option?"

"Our only expeditious one. No one wants me as president—well, not anyone sane—and half the regional governors in the system are new to me. I don't know where their true loyalties lie, nor what they might have been complicit in over the past decade."

Rika pursed her lips. She'd had the same reservations about the Genevians in power. Finding out who was clean and who was a Nietzschean crony would take time.

Time it seemed they no longer had.

"So how would we do it?" she asked.

*<Oh stars! Are you **finally** agreeing to it?>* her AI asked. *<Is this a dream? Does Niki dream of electric sheep?>*

"What are you talking about?"

<Nevermind,> the AI muttered.

"We don't need to get too formal right off, but an official declaration of you as interim president of New Genevia, and a declaration that the estate on Mount Genevia is the center of government should do for now. We'll also need to announce that you are going to convene a cabinet and soon, probably in a few days."

"OK," Rika nodded, her lips twisting to the side. "I don't see a way around this."

"Really?" Tremon shook his head in disbelief. "I expected you to fight a lot harder."

<*It's Oda,*> Niki explained.

"Yeah," Rika agreed, adding a heartfelt sigh. "I'd even accept being crowned queen to keep him from ending up in charge—if for no other reason than I'd rather fly into a star than take orders from Oda."

"Fair enough."

"Oh, make sure the first cabinet meeting is at least four days out."

"Why four?" Tremon asked.

"Because we're going to have a football game in five."

<*And a parade,*> Niki added.

A rare smile tugged at Tremon's lips, and he pushed off from the table, placing a hand on Rika's shoulder. "See? I knew you were the right woman for the job."

"Well, it wasn't my idea."

"Doesn't matter." He shook his head, still smiling. "You've surrounded yourself with the right people. That's the most important thing any leader can do."

PREPARATION

STELLAR DATE: 05.25.8950 (Adjusted Years)
LOCATION: City of Jague, Belgium
REGION: Genevia System, New Genevian Alliance

Luxom's light was fading in Belgium's skies as Caleb walked through the streets of Jague. The towering buildings obstructed much of the view, but every so often, he caught sight of the western sky awash in reds, yellows, and oranges as the dying light bent around the planet and lit the clouds that lay low on the horizon.

The multitude of skyscrapers within the city further shrouded the light, and the primary source of illumination became the lights lining the streets and the glow from the windows of the towers that surrounded him.

Though he was tangentially aware of the edifices that stood all around, his attention was not on the kilometer-high buildings, but rather on the ground, and the route tomorrow's parade would take. He needed to find the best place to strike.

An amateur might try something simple, like firing a shot from a distant building in an attempt to kill the target from outside Colonel Rika's security footprint.... Caleb might have considered that himself, but he didn't think there was a location to be found within a hundred kilometers that her people weren't watching.

A shadow passed between Caleb and the distant sunset, and he knew by the amount of occlusion that it was a ship in low orbit. By the size of the shadow, it would be none other than the mech's flagship, the *Fury Lance.*

A Nietzschean ship.

Everyone had heard the story by now, the tale of how Rika and her Marauders had flown beneath the cloudtops of a gas giant to seek out a Nietzschean fleet and capture it. Her flagship was chief of those spoils, one of the largest dreadnoughts the Niets had ever built.

Until the *Pinnacle.*

The fact that she flew a Niet ship was just another example of what was wrong with Rika. She had her choice of dozens of vessels, and she'd opted to remain aboard the *Fury Lance.*

"Just further evidence," he said softly, careful not to note what the evidence was, and what it was for.

There were ears everywhere.

He finally arrived at his destination, a small restaurant that served raw fish wrapped in rice and seaweed. A connoisseur would argue that there was a lot more to it than that, but Caleb had tried the food on several occasions, and each time, it had not agreed with him.

However, his goal that evening was not to partake in a meal, but to prepare for the day to come—should what he was looking for indeed be present in the establishment.

He pushed through the door to find himself in a dining room that was not much more brightly lit than the skies outside. A woman led him to a seat, and he ordered a dish that he knew would at least be somewhat palatable.

The woman asked Caleb if he'd like a drink, and he decided that it would be just the thing—after all, what he was planning to do was momentous.

I could do with something to steady my nerves.

He ordered a beer and leant back in his seat, staring out the front window, watching the pedestrians walk past as he waited for the right time to kill the restaurant's staff.

* * * * *

Leslie hated how a peaceful street could often feel more dangerous than a battlefield.

She'd fought in more urban engagements than she cared to remember, on a thousand streets just like the ones running through Jague—except they had been crawling with enemies or littered with corpses.

A thousand streets in a hundred cities, she mused, then decided that adding a zero to those numbers might make them more accurate.

She watched a couple pass her by and realized what made the situation so dangerous.

There was no fear.

In battle, everyone was afraid. Honest civilians were in hiding, and soldiers on both sides exhibited varying levels of anxiety that the current conflict would be their last. That worry, the twitch reflexes, the flight or fight response, it was all a symphony to Leslie. It told her who was a threat and who was not. So far as her comrades were concerned, it told her who she could trust to stay on-mission and who was going to lose their shit at the worst possible moment.

It all made sense to her…but a peaceful street was a minefield.

A cunning enemy could blend into the sea of nonchalance and be almost impossible to spot. Especially when the civilians were all excited for the coming day's celebration.

The end result was that *everyone* felt threatening to Leslie, a notion she knew to be ridiculous, but a notion that took up residence in her mind, nonetheless.

Yeah…some of these people have done terrible things. Maybe some in the name of Genevia, some in the name of Nietzschea. Stars know I've done my share as well.

But somewhere in the crowd was a killer who intended to harm Rika. To assume otherwise was to be a fool.

The remnants of the resistance's spy network had heard chatter that there was a bounty on Rika's head. It wasn't much more than rumor, and no one knew who was offering the bounty, or even how to collect, should someone succeed. Even so, Leslie had to take it seriously.

Security forces were scouring the route, but she'd brought in the big guns and asked Piper, the once-multinodal AI that was now the ship's AI aboard the *Fury Lance,* to quietly sift through the city's comm traffic while she walked the parade route.

Leslie had carried out her fair share of hits in the past. It wasn't something she was proud of, not even a little bit. But it did give her an advantage: she knew how to think from a killer's point of view.

Somewhere along the parade route was the perfect place to kill Rika, and she was going to find it.

Of course, the problem Leslie had encountered was that there were *many* excellent places to make a strike against the parade, though most would be easily mitigated by additional security—which she had organized. What she needed to find was the location an enemy would think they'd miss.

She had been patrolling the route for several hours, and it was well past midnight—not that one could tell, from the number of people on the streets. The city had the atmosphere of a giant party. From conversations she'd overheard, a lot of Jague's residents, as well as the sizable number of visitors, had no intention of finding their beds before watching the parade in the morning.

Though their presence made her job more difficult, Leslie didn't begrudge them their celebrations and libations. Liberating systems from the Nietzscheans was the goal, and there was every reason in the universe to celebrate the victories.

Noticing an alcove where an overhead walkway crossed high above the street, Leslie assigned another stealthed Marauder to the position. So far, she had designated watch points for fifty of her best SMI and RR mechs. The enemy would have to get very lucky to have better than a one-in-five-hundred chance of even getting close to Rika.

However, she still hadn't identified that perfect spot. The spot where *she'd* make a strike.

Her patrol had taken her almost to the end of the route, just a few kilometers from the stadium where the football game was to be held after the parade was complete. It was the section of the route where she most expected an attack to occur. Security would have grown complacent, and the human tendency to think that because nothing bad *had* happened, that nothing bad *would* happen would be gaining ground in their minds.

Retracing her steps for the dozenth time, she stopped and closed her eyes for a moment, losing her current orientation of where she'd come from and where she was going, instead allowing herself to simply *be* where she was. It was a tactic she'd learned long ago to reframe her thinking and reevaluate a location as a destination rather than a part of a route.

With fresh eyes, she began to rescan the street. She looked at the shops lining the road, all in good repair, and the towers rising above, each stretching as high as a kilometer, with landing pads hanging off the sides and skyways stretching between the buildings.

Those were less of a concern for her. A grav shield would follow the parade, keeping them safe from above—or at least, safe enough that any single kill shot wouldn't prove fatal. Not only that, but the *Asora* and a wing of skyscreams would be nearby, keeping the skies safe.

All of that meant that if there was a threat, it would come from the ground, an attack from within the crowd, or from one of the storefronts.

It would have to be a hell of an attack to meet with success.

Rika would be marching through the streets with M company, the mechs who had been together since she'd been given her command.

Anything short of an army sent against those four platoons of mechs won't last longer than a few minutes.

Which meant that a successful attack would have to be fast, devastating, and decisive.

The other obvious angle was the maze of tunnels that lay beneath the streets. Drones were already sweeping the subterranean passages, searching for anyone and anything that should not be there. Leslie was following their updates, though not reviewing things too closely.

Piper was handling the detailed analysis, the AI's ability to effectively multitask far superior to her own. The drones would continue to scour the tunnels before and during the parade.

It was getting close to dawn, and Leslie was near the end of the route. Once again, she closed her eyes and went through the steps to see the street around her as though it was entirely unknown to her.

As she scanned the storefronts, something caught her attention. One of the restaurants that had been open the last time she'd passed by was now closed.

She checked their posted schedule and saw that they'd initially planned to stay open all night. However, a new notice on their feed indicated that the early closure was in preparation for the parade, but the lights were off and there was no sign of activity.

It was not what she would have expected from an establishment getting ready for a large influx of customers.

Her survey of the surrounding area continued without her giving any indication that something had registered as out of the ordinary. Once it was complete, she walked to the next intersection and rounded the corner. Two blocks later, she reached an intersection where a group of pedestrians waited to cross the street. She eased into their midst, and when the group began to move, she waited till most of them had passed her by before crouching. Just as the last of the pedestrians walked past her, Leslie activated her stealth systems and rose.

Now invisible—and hopefully unnoticed—she quickly moved to the edge of the group and began to carefully navigate the sidewalks back to the mysteriously closed restaurant.

As she went, she wondered what would have happened if Rika hadn't brought her mechs to the Albany System at the same time as the Intrepid Space Force. The ISF had been there to rescue their leader, Tanis Richards, and Rika had joined in to help, partially out of guilt from her part in the Nietzschean attack on Thebes that had occurred a year earlier.

Even before that mission, Leslie had modified her body with its current cat-like alterations, but she'd not had the stealth abilities the ISF had provided her, abilities she had immediately fallen in love with.

Over the years, she'd encountered many types of flow armor, thin layers of armor that were normally soft and pliable, but would harden on impact. Their effectiveness varied, but none was as good as actual armor with ablative plating.

The ISF's flow armor was better than any light armor Leslie had ever worn, and as good as medium, non-powered gear. But that wasn't even the best part—at least so far as she was concerned. The armor also provided near-perfect invisibility. You could stand right in front of someone who was wearing it and never see them. Only dust or wind blowing around the person would give away their presence—but even that was hard to detect with the armor's visual compensators.

And if all that wasn't enough, the ISF had worked out a

way to simply replace a person's skin with the armor, so that one was never without protection.

All of the mechs had opted for that—especially since they were already used to not having real skin. Leslie had also jumped at the chance. The flow armor was capable of changing color and texture, but Leslie kept hers jet black, to suit her cat-like stealth.

A man suddenly cut left around a pair of women and nearly collided with Leslie. She managed to dodge out of the way just in time, but her tail slapped one of the women on the ass. The woman turned to the man, telling him to keep his hands to himself, to which he protested innocence.

A giggle almost escaped Leslie, but she held it in, thankful that she hadn't crashed into anyone.

That was the thing entertainment vids never showed about stealth: how hard it was to move through crowded areas. In many respects, using a disguise to hide in plain sight was better than full stealth because people could see and avoid you.

Despite her need to weave through the crowds and jump to avoid collisions more than once, Leslie managed to reach the restaurant without further incident and stepped up to the window to peer inside.

What she saw heightened her suspicions further: two tables weren't cleared, and the floor did not appear to be swept. Any eatery that closed early to prepare for crowds the following day would at least clean up properly before leaving for the night.

Leslie pulled up the schematics for the building the restaurant occupied, looking for anything interesting about its location. Nothing jumped out at her. It didn't have a route into the tunnels below the street, or any privileged access into the skyscraper that rose above.

<Piper,> she reached out to the AI high above in the *Fury*

Lance. *<Do you see anything noteworthy about this restaurant?>*

<Other than the fact that their menu seems overpriced for food they didn't even have to cook?>

<Funny, Piper. Yes, other than that.>

The AI didn't respond for nearly a minute, then finally said, *<There just might be.>*

<Well, don't leave me in suspense. What is it?>

<That restaurant is over an old underground maglev access point. According to city records, it's all sealed up now, but it's possible that one person's 'sealed up' is another person's slap-dash job.>

<Slap dash?> Leslie chuckled. *<I like that.>*

<I learned it from Niki. She's quite the repository of esoteric information.>

That wasn't surprising. Niki was possibly one of the oldest AIs in the galaxy—especially in continual time spent out of stasis. How she'd ended up in a position to run into team Basilisk in the Oran System still set Leslie wondering from time to time.

Granted, she'd since learned that there were even older AIs living in the galactic core, so somehow that made running into a being as ancient as Niki a bit less mind-blowing.

A little bit.

<Are you going to check it out?> Piper asked.

<Well yeah, I kind of have to.>

<How are you going to get in? If an enemy is working inside, it might be a bit obvious when the front door opens.>

Leslie had already considered that. *<I can send in drones, disable any monitoring.>*

<That'll take a while.>

<Which is why I'm going to check around back first.>

The restaurant's rear entrance was situated within the building that housed it. The structure's main door was a dozen meters to Leslie's left, and she walked over to it and waited until a man walked in through the revolving door, then followed closely after.

Once inside, she skirted around the security arches, glad that the active scan the building ran was not capable of detecting her stealthed form. From there, she entered the tower's main foyer, taking in the sweeping lines designed to draw the eye upward. A glance at the ceiling revealed that there wasn't one; a kilometer overhead, open sky loomed, ringed by the building's glass and steel.

She drew her gaze away, focusing on her task of getting into the restaurant. There was no public entrance for it from inside the tower, which suited Leslie well enough. It meant there were fewer ways for anyone to escape, should she find someone up to no good.

Piper's schematic of the building led her across the foyer and into a large hall on the right. She followed it for a short time before coming to a maintenance passage. The door was locked, but it didn't take long for her breach kit to work its magic and gain access.

<I could have just hacked the whole building's security. Though maybe that's overkill,> Piper commented as Leslie's drones tapped into the nearby cameras and overrode their datastreams, masking all sign of the door that seemed to open and close on its own.

The maintenance corridor was clean and well lit, but not as well appointed as the passage without. She followed it to the first intersection, and then turned right, coming to a single door at the end bearing the restaurant's name.

Once again, she set her breach kit on the lock system, while threading a filament of nano around the jamb, getting a view of a short hall lined with boxes.

<Feels like cheating,> Leslie commented to Piper. *<I'm so used to breaching secure facilities on ships and stations, planet-side stuff*

is easy to get through.>

<I've noticed that, as well,> the AI replied. *<I wonder if it's because they feel like being on the ground makes them safer. In space, we are constantly thinking three-dimensionally.>*

<Maybe,> Leslie said as she completed her breach. *<Except that in a city like this, 'ground level' is really just a façade on top of its infrastructure.>*

<Perception is nine tenths of reality,> Piper intoned. *<Granted, that's a saying I can only understand through observing humans, but it seems to hold true.>*

<It's true for you too,> Leslie said as she slowly opened the restaurant's rear door. *<You just can't view the abstract one tenth, so you think that perception is always all there is to reality.>*

<That doesn't make any sense.>

<Sure it does. Because you can't perceive abstract incongruities, you think that your observations of reality are not just perception, but ***actual*** *reality.>*

<I can perceive incongruities.> Piper sounded annoyed. *<Sensors, whether they be your eyes or high-resolution optics, all have errors in their functionality. That creates the same sort of noise in the data that makes up your one tenth of reality that does not match perception.>*

<Huh.>

Leslie had never considered the error rates in sensor data to be analogous to the disparity in perception that humans experienced.

Granted, I've never dissected that particular statement before. That's what I get for using figures of speech with an AI like Piper. He hasn't been around people enough not to take everything literally.

She pulled her thoughts back to focus on the task at hand. The restaurant's rear hall was dimly lit, but that wasn't a problem for Leslie. Her night vision was second to none, and she easily worked her way around the clutter, listening for any sounds.

She reached the doorway that led into the kitchen and saw that it was clean and orderly, but there were a few ingredients still on the counters, a clear sign that things had shut down in a hurry.

<*Maybe they just had to go somewhere,*> Piper said, his view coming from the drones that Leslie had released.

<*Sure, could be nothing.*> Her response carried a hefty dose of doubt.

Upon further consideration, Leslie hoped it *was* nothing. She hated the idea that someone would try to kill Rika on a day of celebration.

<*You watching the drone feeds?*> Piper asked, flagging one of the visuals on Leslie's HUD. <*Check it out.*>

Leslie focused on it and saw that the door to a walk-in cooler was open, and in the floor of the refrigeration unit was a rather large hole leading down into a tunnel below.

<*Stars. This is why we can't have nice things.*>

FORCED MARCH

STELLAR DATE: 05.25.8950 (Adjusted Years)
LOCATION: City of Jague, Belgium
REGION: Genevia System, New Genevian Alliance

"Whose idea was this, anyway?" Rika asked as she stood at the hotel room's window, looking out over the city of Jague. "A parade? Seriously?"

Chase snorted as he looked over her armor. "Pretty sure it was the old lady's brilliant plan."

"Well, she's a dumbass. Why would we do what she says?"

"Beats me." Chase walked back around Rika and placed his hands on her shoulders. "She usually has solid plans, but this one? I dunno."

"Woooow." Rika shook her head, the corners of her eyes crinkling as she tried not to laugh. "Just throw her into the engine wash. I see how it is."

"It's going to be a good day." Chase slid his hands from her shoulders to her back, pulling their armored bodies into an embrace. "The parade and game are going to start a tradition that will become important for our people. You'll see."

Rika leant her head against his. "Everything I do is noteworthy now, isn't it?"

A laugh burst from Chase's lips, his chest heaving in the bit of space between their bodies. "Probably not *everything*. You snored a bit last night, but I don't think that'll make the news feeds."

She was tempted to give him a light slap, but her plans were foiled when he released her and backed out of range. Instead, she issued a mock-warning.

"Well, if I do see it on the feeds, I'll know who to blame."

"Mmmhmm." Chase nodded sagely. "Barne."

Rika rolled her eyes and then held out her left arm. Chase took it, and they strode across the mainspace to the room's door. Before they reached it, the portal swung wide to reveal Kelly and her team waiting for them in the hall. Rika nodded as they formed up.

"You ready to watch the ISF Marines get their asses kicked on the field of battle?" Kelly voiced the words with a predatory grin on her lips.

"Umm…am I allowed to express a preference?" Rika asked. "Seems dangerous."

"Dangerous?" Shoshin's posture stiffened. "Dangerous would be not screaming your head off every time the Marauders—and *only* the Marauders—score a goal."

"Don't worry," Rika chuckled. "I know how this works. I still have to be polite to the Marines, though."

"I think that some of Admiral Carson's vacuum jockeys are in on it as well," Chase said. "He holds games on his ships a lot, from what I hear."

"Bringing in ringers," Shoshin muttered. "I see how it is."

Kelly nodded for Keli to secure the lift as they approached the end of the hall before glancing at Rika. "Must be rough being in his command. Even more 'hurry up and wait' than is normal for a service. They just hang out at Albany, waiting for the next emergency that they have to run off and deal with."

"I hope you're not complaining," Chase laughed at the dark-haired woman. "His waiting game has saved our bacon more than a few times."

"I would never complain about Carson," Kelly said with a wink. "Not even a little bit. That guy makes grizzled veterans look like shiny-armored FNMs."

"He seems pretty clean-cut to me," Keli said, casting Kelly a puzzled look as the lift arrived and the doors opened.

"Well, *Admiral* Carson is," Kelly said, a smirk on her lips as the lift doors opened, and Keli quickly checked the car over.

"But he wasn't always an admiral. He used to be TSF, you know."

"Wait," Keli shot Rika a look that suggested she needed a second opinion, while waving the group into the lift. "Admiral Carson was in the Transcend's military? That doesn't make any sense."

"No," Rika shook her head. "Don't forget that the Sol System used to call their military the 'Terran Space Force'. Carson was a fighter pilot in their fleets for years."

"Right," Kelly took over again. "He wanted to keep being a vac jock too, but Tangel promoted him all the way up to admiral and put him in charge of the Fan Fleet."

" 'Fan Fleet'? As in 'shit hits the'?" Chase asked.

Kelly nodded. "I think he just calls it that privately, though."

"Privately?" Shoshin asked, fixing Kelly with a penetrating stare. "Are you banging the ISF admiral?"

"Damn skippy I am. Well, not 'ing', exactly. It was just once—well, one *night*. We did it more than once. The guy has staminaaaaa."

Rika wondered if Shoshin was going to say anything further. The man was very protective when it came to Kelly and Keli. It was a strange dynamic that their team had, but it worked.... It was part of the reason why Sergeant Crunch had advocated that their fireteam not get a fourth member.

Theirs was a comradery that Rika understood all too well; her first fireteam had also consisted of just three mechs. One of them being Kelly.

"Should shift you over to Leslie's group," Chase muttered in response to the woman, a smile pulling at the corners of his lips. "You'd be great at espionage."

Kelly gave the captain a look of pure innocence. "Who's to say that I haven't already done a bit of work for her? On the side, so to speak."

"That really sounds like a euphemism," Keli giggled.

Chase joined in with a laugh. "Double entendrephamism."

"OK, people," Rika managed to speak around the smile splitting her face. "Game faces. There will be feed drones watching us from here on out."

The lift doors opened, and with smooth precision, the two Kellies exited the lift car, their GNRs held across their chests as they strode between the two rows of mechs lined up in the hotel lobby. Chase and Rika followed them out, walking side by side, and the two hundred mechs in attendance saluted sharply, the action punctuated by the sound of their heels—or rear foot claws, in many cases—slapping together.

"Present arms!" Barne's voice thundered through the lobby, and the mechs raised their primary weapons into the air, creating an arch that the pair, followed by Shoshin, strode beneath.

Beyond the mechs stood a host of dignitaries, hotel guests, and what staff had managed to pause for a peek at the leader of the force that had liberated the Genevia System.

Rika could make out a wide variety of attendees. Everyone from wealthy merchants to local police chiefs were present in the crowd, each watching her with hawk-like eyes as she walked toward the front doors and the sunlit street beyond.

A fear crept into her mind that something terrible was going to happen the moment she stepped onto the street, but when she strode into the early morning light, there was nothing to see—or fear—than more crowds of people, these ones held back by drones and local Jague police.

She noted that on her left, two B'muths stood idle, ready to form the rear of the procession, so she turned to the right, staring down the long stretch of road.

<*Just nine kilometers to our destination,*> Niki advised.

Rika sighed. <*Gonna feel like we're fighting Niets the whole way.*>

<*Why's that?*>

<*Because.*> Rika approached Admiral Carson, who was waiting on the street. <*We have to walk…I can't remember the last time I just walked through a city.*>

"Colonel Rika," Carson extended his hand as the Marines arrayed behind him drew up and saluted her. "The ISF is honored that you're including us in your celebration."

Rika clasped Carson's hand in her own, giving it two firm shakes as she replied, "The Genevian people are forever in the ISF's debt. We would still be living under Nietzschean rule if it were not for you."

Carson smiled, and Rika looked around at the crowds lining the streets. Most people were clapping and cheering, but some looked worried, their expressions pensive.

Rika knew what they were worried about, and she decided that a march through the streets of Jague amidst a doubtful populace was not how she wanted to start the day.

Time to change tactics.

With a few quick strides and a boost from her a-grav system, she leapt into the air and landed atop the foremost B'muth's head. She turned toward the assembled crowds and clamped her feet around a groove in the massive walker's armor while tapping into its public address systems.

"People of Jague!" Her voice thundered from the speakers, silencing the crowds. "People of Belgium, People of Genevia! I stand here before you not as a conqueror, not as a victor on the field of battle, but as a sister, as a daughter of Genevia."

<*Ohh…now that's a great opening,*> Niki said privately.

<*Hush…don't trip me up.*>

"I know that many of you wonder what having so many mechs come to Genevia might mean. Seeing us together like this makes you worry that we're angry, that we'll exact revenge for what was done to us, that the strength we displayed in fighting the Nietzscheans will be turned against you.

"Let me tell you now that you have nothing to fear from us. We know that the people had nothing to do with our mechanization, but even those who *did* perpetrate these crimes against us are forgiven. We will not seek any punitive measures.... We only seek acceptance from our people."

A ripple of surprise flowed through the crowds, and Rika saw her mechs stand a little straighter.

She'd not spoken to them about her decision not to seek reparations. She hadn't needed to. No mech saw themselves as a victim; they considered what had happened in the first war with Nietzschea to be the crucible that forged them into the exact weapon that the people of Genevia needed.

"We are your sons and daughters, your brothers and sisters. We have come home to you with a gift. The gift of freedom. Not only that, but we will bring this gift to *all* of Genevia, until we see every last member of our great extended family, our people, liberated from Nietzschea!"

For a moment, there was silence, and Rika feared that she'd misspoken somehow, but then the crowd roared in response, and she stood tall, masking the relief she felt, knowing that she'd struck the right tone.

"But before we lift the chains of oppression across old Genevia, we're going to strike at the enemy's heart. The next system we strike is going to be Nietzschea itself. Emperor Constantine is dead, but his empire will live on—unless we put it down like the sick beast that it is.

"So join us today in celebrating a momentous victory against the Niets, join with us as we honor those who gave their lives for our freedom, and stand with us as we thank our allies, Admiral Carson and the ISF—right before we crush them on the football field!"

Rika hadn't even finished her statement when the crowd began to cheer so loudly that even her amplified words were drowned out. Capitalizing on the excitement, she gave word for the procession on the street below to begin their march.

<*You going to ride up there?*> Chase asked from where he stood smiling up at her.

<*Umm…should I?*>

<*Absolutely. You look every bit the queen.*>

<*Oh not you too.*>

The only response she received was a laugh, and then Chase turned to walk next to Admiral Carson, the two men's heads bent together in conversation.

A moment later, the B'muth began to move, and Rika checked on who the operator was.

<*Lieutenant Carson? What are you doing in there?*>

<*Driving a B'muth. What did you think I was doing?*>

<*Funny.*>

The man the mechs all called Bondo laughed. <*Well,* **I** *thought it was. In all honesty, this 'Muth is a bit twitchy. It took some hits in a fight last week. I've got most of the kinks ironed out, but I figured it would be wise to have me at the helm just in case it goes sideways.*>

<*You mean if something goes wrong with it?*> Niki asked.

<*No, I mean literally sideways, as in careens through the crowd and then slams into a building.*>

<*Shit,*> Rika muttered. <*Didn't we have another 'Muth?*>

<*Sure…on Capeton. You didn't give a lot of notice for this little soiree, and Barne wanted two.*>

Rika held back a sigh as the walker continued to trundle forward. The mechs didn't often rely on B'muths, dropping them only when they needed to bring overwhelming firepower in short order. Mostly it was because the walkers weren't much deadlier than a pair of determined K1R mechs, and made for larger targets.

<You look good up there,> Chase said from below. *<Keep it up.>*

<I'm just standing here and waving.>

<And not falling off.>

Rika snorted. *<I just wish I were wearing a helmet. I'm starting to feel like there's a target on my forehead.>*

<The 'Muth has a grav shield up.>

<Yeah, I know.>

She still felt vulnerable. That was the first rule of the battlefield: take your helmet off only if you want to die.

She just had to convince herself that Jague wasn't a battlefield. It was a friendly city.

Well, mostly friendly.

* * * * *

Caleb rechecked the device, double-checking the magnetic shielding and the hard-Link cable that ran into the networking trunkline. The last thing he wanted was to go to all this trouble only to have a comm issue derail everything.

Especially because I won't get a second chance if things misfire—at least not a shot this easy.

Though he was confident he could take out the Marauder leadership in the parade, Caleb wondered if his benefactors had overestimated the disruption their deaths would cause. From what he'd learned about the mercenary organization, there was a strong chain of command—much of it still aboard their ships. There was no reason to believe that they wouldn't be able to operate in Rika's absence.

Not only that, but Admiral Carson of the ISF was present. It was entirely possible that if he died, his people would have a strong reaction—and not the sort Caleb's employers wanted to see. He had expressed those concerns, but they were noted and then overruled.

Well, I get paid either way, he thought as the device checks came back clean.

Satisfied that no one would spot it with scan or on the net, he proceeded to give it one last visual inspection.

The bomb he'd devised was simple: four grams of antimatter held in a containment vessel. He'd send the signal to disable the field holding the antimatter, and it would fall into a block of uranium.

People often thought that it was easy to make an antimatter bomb. In theory, it was. There was no chance of a misfire; as soon as antimatter touched matter, annihilation and destruction would ensue. The tricky part was the risk of diffusion.

When the first atoms of antihydrogen hit any normal matter, the explosion would fling out the remaining antihydrogen atoms. Some of those atoms would move a good distance before hitting other matter and annihilating it.

Normally that wasn't a problem, but he needed to ensure that the bulk of the blast went upward and tore through the road in order to kill the mechs. To facilitate that blast shape, the antimatter in his bomb was stretched into a film that was just a few atoms thick. When it fell toward the block of uranium, the sheet of antimatter would hit the dense uranium atoms simultaneously. Or close enough to make no difference.

If it worked as well as he expected, the bomb would create a sizable crater in the center of the city.

Caleb rose and gave the meter-high oval one last check, testing that it was secure and perfectly level. As he stepped back and surveyed his work with approval, an alert caught his attention, and he pulled up a feed of the restaurant above.

There had been motion in the back hall, but from what the restaurant's visual feeds showed, there was no one present.

Granted, they hadn't sent the alert; it had come from Caleb's own equipment, a carefully calibrated sensor that detected vibrations in the floor.

It had given several false positives through the night, which had been expected. Isolating vibrations in a large building in the middle of a busy city was no simple task. So he'd dutifully checked the restaurant each time it had triggered, and each time, the restaurant had been completely empty.

He was tempted to ignore the alert now, especially given that the parade had begun, and he needed to get outside of the blast radius, but at the same time, if his bomb was found, all his work would be for nothing, and a future attack would be far more difficult.

He backed out of the shadowed alcove in the long-abandoned service tunnel. Once out of the narrow space, he pulled the steel cabinet back into place and then dusted himself off before pulling his stealth cloak on.

Caleb knew it wouldn't hide him as well as the mechs or the ISF Marines, but he didn't need it to shroud him in full sunlight, just in the subterranean corridors. In addition, the cloak only needed to hide him long enough to get the drop on whoever was snooping around.

That's what he told himself, at least.

In reality, he knew that his chances of spotting a stealthed enemy were slim to none. It was more likely that they'd physically run into one another.

"Shit," Caleb muttered, arriving at the inescapable conclusion that he needed to remain near the bomb until he was either certain that the alert had been triggered in error, or the investigator entered the tunnels and he could figure out how to take them down.

And then hope I can still get away before the bomb goes off…or scrub the mission entirely.

Given the nature of his benefactors, if he walked away from the job, he would need to get out of the Genevia System and find someplace far away to restart his career—something he wasn't prepared to do just yet.

Four minutes. If no one comes into the tunnel by then….

With pursed lips and a decision made, he deployed a flight of microdrones, directing some to activate a Link suppressor before backing into a shadowy alcove to begin his wait.

* * * * *

Leslie eased down through the hole and into the passage below. It had taken some time to find all the sensors monitoring the opening—or at least, what she hoped were all of them—before it had been safe to proceed.

Even so, she had to assume that whoever was operating below the restaurant was expecting her.

Leslie instructed Piper to alert Rika that she suspected a bomb—she couldn't think of what else it could be—beneath the road at the restaurant's location.

The AI hadn't confirmed that the message made it through to Rika before Leslie had gone EM-silent, but she wasn't worried. Piper could be trusted to let them know not to pass this way until Leslie gave the all-clear.

The moment her feet hit the tunnel floor, she eased to the side of the space and looked over the debris left from the hole's opening, scanning for signs of how many people might be in the tunnels with her.

Unfortunately, once she moved past the dust and rubble, there was no sign of anyone having been in the passage at all.

Track sweeper, she thought, looking at the evenly distributed dust that appeared to have been settling for decades.

She didn't have any such equipment, and left light

footprints in the dust as she moved in the direction of the street, assuming that if there was a bomb, it would be positioned directly under the parade route.

After a dozen meters, the dark passage rounded a corner and met another unlit tunnel that led in the direction of the street.

She followed it as quickly and quietly as she could, finally reaching a passage that ran lengthwise beneath the road above. It was wider than the others, almost four meters across, and five high. From where Leslie stood, she could see a dozen alcoves and side-passages that ran off it.

Well, crap, she thought, looking for any sign of her prey.

No sound came from above—and she was certain that a company of mechs and 'Muths would be easily heard in the tunnels—and she grew certain that the parade had diverted.

Leslie turned to the right and flushed out a nanocloud, sending it in a wide spread ahead of her. Time was now on her side, her primary goal shifting to the capture of whoever was operating down here. She wanted to find out if they were working alone, or at someone else's behest.

She moved as quickly as she dared, watching the feeds from her drones as she advanced. Her probes spotted a pipe that appeared to have been scratched recently, and she moved toward it, but by the time she arrived, the drones found that it was still connected to the water mains and liquid was flowing unimpeded.

Several other false positives distracted Leslie until she was sixty meters from where she'd entered the tunnel. A dark passage led off on her left, and while the dust on the floor was undisturbed, there was a handprint on the wall that told a different tale.

It wasn't a smoking gun, but her nanoprobes picked up a small amount of oil in the handprint, its viscosity indicating that the print had been deposited there within the last day.

Leslie let the nanocloud move down the side passage, the drones sniffing for any signs of a bomb while she followed a few meters behind. She was beginning to suspect that whoever had come down into the tunnels was long gone—either that, or they were lying in wait for her.

Let them try, she thought with a smirk.

The smirk faded as her nano finally saw another sign, a scrape on the floor near an equipment rack. It was fresh, and there was no doubt that it had been moved within the past day.

About time, I—

The thought faded away as the probes flew around the rack and showed a meter-high oval sitting in the darkened alcove.

From the outside, Leslie had no idea what it was, but the device's size alone was troubling enough. Her first thought was that it could be a nuke, but her probes weren't detecting any radiation.

Pulling the rack aside, she crouched down next to the device, noting that a hard-Link cable ran from it through a small hole in the wall. The blueprints of the area indicated that there was a network trunkline on the other side of the wall, meaning that the physical connection was likely in place both to detect tampering and to enable remote activation.

Checking the time, Leslie saw that the parade was only a few minutes away, though the procession would be two blocks to the east on the first alternate route. Those two blocks had been an ample detour when she thought that it was a small explosive. What she was looking at now could be a nuclear bomb, or something far worse. The concern that it might be an antimatter device took root in her mind.

A quick calculation told her that if she were dealing with antimatter, the device's yield could drop the skyscrapers linking the road above. Given that they were each a kilometer high, the alternate parade route was well within the destructive zone.

Throwing caution to the wind, she initiated a relay chain through her probes and reached out for help.

<Piper? I think we have a bigger problem than I thought.>

She waited several seconds, getting no reply. Then her drones picked up a change in the air currents behind her.

* * * * *

<Piper, have you heard anything further from Leslie?>

<No, Rika, not since her final message that she was going EM-silent.>

The battalion of mechs ahead of Rika had already begun to turn onto the road that would take them down the alternate parade route. On the sidewalks—and parts of the street—crowds of onlookers were streaming onto the new road in order to get a better look at the procession.

No word from Leslie at this point was expected, but Rika still didn't like it.

<Why can't things ever go smoothly?> she asked Niki.

<Because then anyone could do it.>

<Wouldn't that be nice,> Rika replied before reaching out to Silva. *<Major, I want two fireteams in those tunnels backing Leslie up, with the rest of their squad up top.>*

She didn't explain which tunnels were on her mind, but Silva didn't ask, either.

<On it, Colonel. I've been feeling a bit antsy about Leslie's little discovery as well.>

<What's with all the ants lately?>

<Pardon?>

<Nevermind. Just get them over there fast.>

<Don't worry, Rika.> Silva's tone had switched to the motherly one she used to use when she ran Team Hammerfall.

<I'm going to worry anyway, kay?> Rika told her.

<I would too.>

The B'muth began to turn to the right, following the new route, when it lurched left and stopped moving.

<Sorry, Colonel,> Lieutenant Carson called up. *<Wish you'd chosen the alternate route that only involved left-hand turns.>*

<You want the parade route that just goes in circles?> she asked.

<Yeah, that would be perfect.... OK, compensated. Here we go.>

The B'muth started up again, moving to the right and navigating the turn as gracefully as the lumbering machine could.

<Niki?>

<Yes, Rika?>

<This is wrong. We shouldn't be doing this.>

<Doing what?> the AI asked. *<Should we move to the other alternate route?>*

<No.> Rika shook her head. *<We're running, we're on the defensive. This not how we operate.>*

<For starters, it's a parade, not a fleet maneuver. You're being smart, avoiding a threat.>

<That's just the thing, we don't avoid threats.>

The AI snorted. *<OK, well, you're not exactly avoiding it. You sent a squad to deal with it. You just hate missing out on the action.>*

As much as Rika hated to hear it, she suspected that Niki was right. Her life had progressed to the point where not only did she send mechs into danger while she was safe, she did it while riding a B'muth in a parade.

* * * * *

Caleb watched the data rolling in from his sensors with a

single-minded intensity. Twice now, he'd caught errant wind currents, but when he crosschecked the scans, nothing showed up. If there was an enemy moving through the tunnel, it would imply stealth tech that could alter air movement.

Theoretically, it wasn't impossible for a stationary object to do that, but to move *and* mask air currents was an ability he hadn't expected even these more advanced enemies to possess.

Or he was just paranoid and misinterpreting the data.

Eventually, enough time had passed that he decided there was no reason to stay hidden any longer. He'd almost taken his first step out of the alcove, when the equipment rack across the passage shifted, sliding out enough to admit a slim body.

Holy shit…they got within three meters of me, and I can't see a thing!

A small bit of dust shifted on the ground, and he knew that his visitor had moved into the alcove.

Caleb ran through a series of options, one of which was to push the rack onto the intruder and run. As tempting as that was, he knew that was foolish. Mechs and ISF soldiers were modded to the point that an equipment rack landing on them wouldn't buy more than a few seconds. Such a crude approach would also risk breaking the bomb's level-set and reduce the size of the blast.

Moreover, he knew that there was no way he could just sneak away. They would have left probes in the tunnel, and his stealth tech was not good enough to fool physical probes in the air.

There was only one other option. With the utmost care, he reached inside his cloak and felt for the colloid ball. He drew it out so slowly that the speed would have driven a snail mad, and then, when it was free of the cloak, Caleb flicked his wrist, bouncing the ball off the wall and into the alcove. There was a soft *pop*, and he knew the colloid had been delivered.

Let's do this.

He surged forward, but had only taken a single step when a yellow-streaked shape burst out of the alcove and lunged at him.

Caleb—expecting to have been the aggressor—fell back, fumbling for his sidearm, when something struck his left arm, leaving it numb and throbbing. Then a fist slammed into his face, the force dropping him to his ass.

The fall opened up enough room between him and his attacker for Caleb to draw his pistol and aim it at the enemy's center of mass. He squeezed the trigger, and the weapon unleashed a barrage of kinetic rounds interspersed with concussive pulse blasts.

The weapon's kick slammed his elbow back against the ground, but he was pleased to see the shots lift his assailant off the ground and fling her backward. She—he was certain it was a woman, from what he could make of her shape—slammed into the wall and dropped to a knee.

He struggled to his feet, while she remained still.

The weapons fire had shattered the silence he'd been operating in for the last few hours, and that liberated his tongue.

"You're going to regret snooping around down here."

Caleb took a step forward, lifting his gun to fire, when there was a blur of motion, and the woman was suddenly centimeters from him, her hand pushing his weapon to the side.

"No. *You're* going to regret it."

* * * * *

As the rounds from the man's weapon struck her body, Leslie had half a second to think about how big an idiot she was. Knocking him back was just what he'd wanted.

She knew her armor would protect her from whatever a sidearm could deliver, though it hurt like a god's hammer had slammed into her chest, but it took her a moment to shake off the effects.

She watched from beneath hooded eyes as her opponent rose to his feet, also shaking—likely more from adrenaline than the pain of being knocked down.

The man was bringing his weapon to bear again, and she knew that a second barrage was not something she wanted to experience.

He voiced a blustering threat Leslie barely heard before she kicked back and pushed off the wall. She closed the gap between them in an instant, and slammed the heel of her hand into his wrist, pushing his weapon wide.

"No," she hissed. "*You're* going to regret it."

I need to work on my one-liners.

He struggled against her, but her other hand clamped around his neck, and she pushed him back, slamming his outstretched arm into the wall, and breaking his grip on the pistol.

"The bomb, you're going to disable it," she snarled.

A warbling laugh sputtered out of the man's throat. "Well, it wasn't even activated. Until now, that is."

"Aw crap," Leslie muttered. "I was really hoping that you weren't the suicidal type."

"I might not be," he countered. "There's enough time for us to get away. Just let go and—"

"And we let a few thousand people die? What is it, by the way, antimatter?"

"Smart woman," he replied with a rasping laugh. "We've got a few more seconds to get out of here, otherwise we won't make it far enough."

Leslie pursed her lips, wondering if that would even be possible. The man could just be trying to get her away from the device so that she couldn't disable it.

She tried to reach out to Piper through her network of probes again, but wasn't able to make a connection on the far end. Likely, the mad bomber in her clutches had set up some sort of jamming device. She'd directed her drones to extend their reach, stretching their chain into the skyscraper's public corridors in search of a connection, but so far, they'd not gotten back on the Link.

Then the solution came to her, and if she hadn't been grappling with the bomber, she would have slapped herself in the head—metaphorically speaking, of course.

The nano she'd dropped on the bomb was working on infiltrating its systems, running the hack through the device's hard-Link port.

Which was connected to a trunkline.

"C'mon, bitch!" the man swore, beginning to struggle more violently. "We have to go!"

"Nah." Leslie deactivated her stealth so he could see her grin. "We're gonna stay and see what happens. It could be fun!"

While speaking, she routed a connection through the hard-Link cable and reached out to Piper.

<*I have a bomb! It's live!*>

<*Route me to it,*> the AI replied, and Leslie indicated the path and port that connected to the device.

<*Hard-Link, good,*> Piper said and then fell silent.

"Don't worry, we're safe. My AI is going to disable your little party trick," Leslie informed the man. "It was a good try, but now you're going to be up on attempted mass murder charges."

At her words, he ceased struggling. The hood on his cloak had fallen back, revealing a resigned expression on his face.

"You might as well kill me now. That's what'll happen

once I'm in custody."

"Maybe," Leslie said with a shrug. "Maybe not. I doubt that whoever hired you is so well connected that they could infiltrate an ISF cruiser."

A mixture of hope and resignation formed a conflicting expression on the man's face. "Really? I suppose you're right."

"Glad you think so," Leslie replied. "But don't get your hopes up. We could still die down here."

"I'm no martyr," the man said after a moment's pause. "There. The bomb's disabled."

<*Can you confirm that it's offline?*> Leslie asked Piper.

<*It seems to be, though I'm going to make doubly certain.*>

<*I'd appreciate that.*> She returned her focus to the man. "OK, then. Let's start nice and simple. What's your name?"

"Caleb," the man answered. "I—"

His words were cut off as the ground shook beneath their feet. Caleb fell forward, and Leslie had to grab the wall to remain upright.

"What the hell?!" she gasped.

RIKA BOMBA

STELLAR DATE: 05.25.8950 (Adjusted Years)
LOCATION: City of Jague, Belgium
REGION: Genevia System, New Genevian Alliance

<*Klen!*> Captain Heather cried out in Vargo's mind. <*Get the* Asora *in position for a shield extension!*>

<*Shield extension?*> he asked. <*Against what?*>

<*An antimatter bomb! It's situated on the original route. But if it goes—*>

Vargo tuned Heather out as he took helm control from the autopilot and dove his five-hundred-and-forty-four-meter destroyer down toward the planet's surface, threading the needle-like towers, bringing the ship over the alternate parade route.

He summoned an overhead view of the buildings and his ship, pursing his lips in concentration as he brought the *Asora* to within four hundred meters of the ground, the vessel coming to rest directly over the B'muth that Rika stood atop.

<*Colonel, you should get inside the 'Muth,*> he suggested on the command net. <*If that bomb goes off, these buildings could come down.*>

<*Niki and I were just discussing the same thing,*> Rika replied.

<*I have access,*> Piper announced. <*Working on disabling the bomb. Confirmed, it is an antimatter device.*>

<*Shit,*> Chase swore. <*How'd they get antimatter into the city?*>

<*We'll find out later,*> Rika said. <*Vargo, careful up there, you're scratching the paint and scaring the people. The thrumming from your grav engines is bad enough.*>

Vargo shifted the *Asora* a meter to port, moving the ship's starboard aft beam weapon array out of some poor woman's office.

<*Which way are you going, Colonel?*> he asked. <*Back or forward?*>

<*Carson informs me that this 'Muth stands no chance of turning around, so we're going forward.*>

<*Understood.*> Vargo glanced at Chief Ashley. "We're in position. You ready to drop grav shields?"

"No!" Ashley's voice wavered. "I mean…how? Ground's half a klick down! If I extend shields that far, I won't have enough fidelity, someone is gonna get crushed!"

"Get them ready anyway," he replied. "The comp can aim them, just make sure it understands priorities. Rika and the—"

<*Confirmed disarmament,*> Piper announced on the command net, and Vargo sagged in his seat.

<*You're sure?*>

<*I said confirmed, didn't I?*>

Before Vargo could respond, alarms blared, and the shields registered impacts. The holodisplay of the ship and the two towers on either side showed the one on the left sagging against the *Asora* while the destroyer's grav shields pushed against it and the ground, propping the building up.

"Shit!" Ashley cried out. "Fuck! We got pushed over. The shields came down on the walkway!"

"Focus on keeping us from ending up under that tower!" Vargo ordered.

<*There was a second bomb,*> Piper said, his voice filled with lamentation. <*Stars…it wasn't antimatter, just placed perfectly to bring the building down.*>

<*It still might,*> Vargo said. <*The ground is starting to buckle under us. We're gonna find out if the* Asora *can fit in a maglev tunnel.*>

<*We're coming!*> Heather called out. <*Just give us five.*>

Vargo flipped the forward display to show the view below the ship. People were fleeing in every direction, the mechs and

Marines trying to direct civilians down the street and away from the collapsing building.

<Heather, you'd better make that five seconds.>

*****

Rika reached back for the B'muth's access hatch just as the explosion's shockwave hit her. The blast was enough to lift the massive walker a meter into the air, and she lost her footing, tumbling over the side.

With a practiced flip, Rika righted herself and landed on her feet right next to one of the B'muth's legs.

"What the hell?" she shouted both aloud and over the Link.

<There was a second bomb.>

The *Fury Lance*'s ship AI proceeded to inform them that it hadn't been antimatter, but was probably intended to bring down one of the buildings.

Rika looked around the walker's bulk and saw that the kilometer-high tower on the other side of the road was leaning precariously, held up only by the *Asora*'s grav shields.

Good guess.

She spun around and saw a shimmering grav wall just a few meters away, the 'foot' the *Asora* was using to hold up the tower. The sidewalk beneath the grav field was already crushed, and mixed in with the pulverized rubble were the remains of a few bodies. She couldn't tell if they were civilian, mech, or Marine, but knew that wasn't the problem she needed to deal with right then.

She moved toward the front of the walker, calling out on the combat net, *<We need to get these people out of here!>*

Chase stood a few meters away, and glanced back at her, nodding with relief before he resumed disseminating orders over the Link. He directed three squads to get the civilians moving back the direction the parade had come from, while sending one of the mech companies forward to clear a path.

<OK, Carson, get a move on.>

<Ma'am,> the engineer said in what she knew to be his idea tone. *<If Stripes keeps his 'Muth back where it is, and I move forward, we can use our shields to help support the* Asora. *Buy it time until the* Lance *gets in place.>*

Rika looked around and saw that her mechs could get out of the way easily enough, and the civilians who had gathered for the parade would be cleared out in a minute.

The leaning building, on the other hand, had over five thousand people still inside.

<OK, do it.>

Carson's 'Muth lumbered forward, wobbling side to side as he fought to keep it moving in a straight line. Rika tried not to think about what would happen if he lost control and it careened into the building.

<Stars…next time, we need to tell him not to bring a broken walker down for a parade,> Niki commented.

<I guess he was trying to impress the old lady.>

The AI snorted. *<Who, me? That sort of thing doesn't impress me.>*

<You're just a bucket of ha-ha's.>

During their exchange, the groaning from the building had gotten louder, and Rika noted that in another thirty seconds, the civilians on the street would be clear—though a new group was emerging from the building, following the direction of Goob's team, and moving back past Stripes's walker.

Trusting that the situation was in hand as much as it could be, she jogged forward to where Chase and Admiral Carson were directing their troops from just beyond the building's shadow.

"We're as clear as we'll get." Chase still looked concerned as he spoke, his eyes turning up to the leaning building and the starship supporting it.

Admiral Carson whistled. "That sure isn't in the training manual."

Rika nodded mutely, unable to tear her eyes away from the swaying peak of the building, amazed that it hadn't broken apart yet.

<*Bondo, you going to do something magical?*> Vargo asked. <*Because either the* Asora *is about to make a big hole, or we're going to see if we can start a Jague-sized game of dominoes.*>

<*Yeah, slave your shield systems to me,*> Bondo said from the B'muth as it stopped moving. <*I'm going to try to use a resonant frequency to amplify our output.*>

<*Whoa, no, not like that,*> Niki interjected. <*That won't be enough to stabilize the tower, and the top hundred meters will fall off.*>

<*You have a better idea?*>

<*I do,*> the AI said. She proceeded to rapid-fire at the engineer a series of instructions that Rika could barely follow.

<*Shit…*> Bondo swore. <*That'll burn out our systems.*>

<*Probably,*> Niki confirmed. <*But not till after the* Fury Lance *shows up.*>

<*Do it, Bondo,*> Rika ordered. <*Niki practically invented the graviton emitter. She knows her shit.*>

<*She did? Seriously?*>

<*Questions later. Action now!*> Niki ordered.

Everyone fell silent, all eyes on the top of the tower as it continued to sway back and forth. Rika hoped not many people were up that high, and if any were….

Well, I hope they don't have a lot of loose objects around.

As she chastised herself for such a callous thought, the building began to sway less, and the discordant vibrations thrumming through the air decreased.

"Whatever you're doing, it's working," Chase said.

<I can see that,> Niki replied. *<I'm right here too.>*

Chase shot Rika a frustrated look, and she shrugged.

"I guess Niki hates to hear the obvious stated," she told him.

<Just concentrating.>

Rika saw Barne approaching from her left, and the master sergeant cleared his throat when he caught her eye. "I know you like to have a front row seat, but do you think you three can back it up a bit? Or at least not stand in the middle of the road with bullseyes painted on your heads?"

"Shit, yeah," Admiral Carson said. "Sorry. Not used to all this planet-side stuff. Been on ships too long."

"Well, no excuse here," Rika said as she followed Barne across the road to the lee of the next building.

Her anxiety lessened and her breath came easier as the leaning building continued to stabilize. Moments after they reached the relative safety of the next building, Rika saw the *Fury Lance* lower through the clouds, its four-kilometer-long hull dwarfing the *Asora* and the city's skyscrapers.

<Got it,> Piper announced. *<You can unwedge yourself, Vargo.>*

<Gladly,> the captain said, and the *Asora* began to ease backward out of the gap, the side of the ship scraping along the tower on the other side of the road.

<I think you need to get your license to fly that thing examined,> Bondo called up. *<Either that, or it's got a hell of a blind spot.>*

<Says the guy who couldn't drive a 'Muth straight for the life of him.>

*<It's **broken**!>*

Vargo laughed as his ship finally got clear of the building and began to gain altitude. *<Right, sure. That's what they all say.>*

<Rika?> Leslie's voice came over the command net, and Rika breathed a long sigh of relief.

<Stars, Leslie, glad you're OK. You ***are*** *OK, right?>*

<I am, yeah. And I've made a new friend. You're really going to want to hear what he has to say.>

COMING CLEAN

STELLAR DATE: 05.26.8950 (Adjusted Years)
LOCATION: *Fury Lance,* Belgium
REGION: Genevia System, New Genevian Alliance

"You know you can't cut a deal with him, right?" Barne growled as he stared at the man Leslie had captured. "He's a fucking mass murderer."

"Attempted," Rika corrected the master sergeant. "He didn't actually pull it off."

Barne's brow lowered, and he looked like he was going to spit. "Scumbag is too calm. He's done this sort of thing before. Might not have committed *this* massacre, but I bet there's an ocean of blood on his hands."

Rika grimaced, not at the thought of what Caleb might have done, but at the memories that surged to the forefront. She resisted the urge to look down at her own hands and the sea of blood on them.

She placed a hand on his shoulder and gave the man a reassuring look. "I'm not going to set him free. He's going to prison for what he did. Carson offered to take him to the ISF's POW facility if we're worried about someone offing him."

"Someone like me." Barne snorted after voicing the words, then drew a deep breath and closed his eyes. "OK…I think I need to go scream at some FNMs for a bit. That always calms me down."

Rika laughed. "We don't have any FNMs in the Marauders. Unless you want to scream at yourself, Vargo, or Chase. You three are our newest mechs."

"Don't forget about some of the LHO mechs on the ship crews," Barne said with an arched brow.

"Sure, see how Heather responds to you reaming out her

crews. Better yet, film it. I love to watch SMIs take assault mechs down a notch."

The master sergeant blanched. "OK...good point. Even Heather's happy face can be a bit intimidating."

"Yeah, it's why she's such a good fleet commander."

The statement reminded Rika that she needed to reorganize the fleets and lay in a host of promotions. Of course, that meant promoting herself, which she couldn't do so long as she was a Marauder.

Barne nodded. "Can't argue with that. OK, I'm going to leave you to it, see if Leslie needs a hand with her hunt for whoever planted the second bomb."

"Good luck, Master Sergeant."

He tossed her a salute before walking away and calling over his shoulder, "You too, Colonel."

<Niki, have you and David made any headway on our legal tangle?>

A long sigh filled her mind, the tone of which almost made Rika laugh.

<Yes and no. We have a plan to extricate ourselves, but it's stuck in a bit of a catch-22. We hope to have an option for you soon.>

<OK.>

Rika turned back to the wall-filling display of the next room. It showed the man who had nearly detonated an antimatter bomb sitting serenely at the table, his hands folded in front of him. Sensor data on the upper right showed that his bio readouts matched his expression. If he was feeling any stress, he was hiding it very well.

<Barne's handling this well,> the AI said after a moment, interrupting Rika's observations. *<I thought he'd fly off the handle more than he has.>*

<Oh?> Rika wondered what Niki was getting at. *<I didn't notice anything out of character.>*

<No? You need to read between the lines. He was freaking out about Leslie almost dying.>

"Huh," Rika said aloud. *<OK, I guess I wasn't thinking that way. But Leslie has been in dozens of dangerous situations since she and Barne became an item. Why would this one faze him more than the others?>*

<I think it's because she was alone,> Niki suggested.

<Leslie has always worked on her own. It's sort of her thing. She's changed herself into a black panther, for goodness sakes. That's a pretty big 'I go it alone' statement.>

The AI laughed at Rika's statement and then added a sigh. *<That's what makes it so hard for Barne, I think. He loves how strong and independent she is, but he never opens himself up to anyone, you know that. I bet that since he's done it with Leslie, he really worries about losing her and the connection they've made.>*

<We'd all be devastated if we lost Leslie,> Rika countered.

<Of course we would. You know no good comes from trying to measure who has more misery—especially potential misery. I'm just bringing this up to explain why he's extra twitchy, not to say he has some sort of monopoly on worry about Leslie.>

Rika pursed her lips, nodding slowly. "OK, I get that. And now I'm going to put it out of my mind so I can focus on this dickwad."

As she finished her sentence, the door behind her opened, admitting Commandant Perin, head of the Jague Police Department, and a woman Rika's HUD identified as Detective Kora.

"I assume you're talking about our guest, Colonel?" the man said.

Rika extended a hand, which the captain clasped. "Commandant Perin, good to see you. And yeah, I was just getting out some frustration before going in."

"You're planning on speaking to him yourself?" the woman asked, then flushed. "Sorry, Colonel Rika, I'm

Detective Kora."

"Nice to meet you, detective," Rika shook the woman's hand. "And yes, I was. I find that people often become quite talkative in a mech's presence."

"OK..." Kora drew the word out. "I just feel like we should work him a bit. Taking him up here to your ship has already made him feel more important, like he's in a solid bargaining position. If you go in first thing, then he'll know that he has all the power in the situation."

Rika pursed her lips, nodding slowly. "OK. I see your point, I'm not used to being the big boss lady, but I guess that's the way it is now."

Commandant Perin and the detective shared a look of relief at Rika's words, and she cocked an eyebrow.

"Well, don't think I won't come in if it's warranted," she told them.

"Oh, it'll probably be warranted at some point," Detective Kora smirked. "Let's just use it for maximum effect."

Rika nodded, and gestured to the full-wall display. "OK, the show is yours."

The outline of a door appeared, and the detective walked toward it, glancing over her shoulder at the other two before she pushed it open. "I assume there are security measures in the room?"

"There are," Rika replied. "His mods are all disabled, and there's a sleepy-time packet at the base of his neck. If he so much as blinks sideways, he'll be out like a light."

Kora gave a toothy grin. "Awesome."

She opened the door and passed through, its outline fading once it closed behind her. The display now showed Kora walking to the table and sitting across from Caleb, the man barely registering acknowledgment of her presence.

The detective seemed nonplussed by the lack of reaction,

and dragged her chair back and to the side. She settled into it and put her booted feet on the table, tilting the chair back as though she hadn't a care in the world.

"Quite the performance already," Rika commented to the commandant.

"She's good. One of our best," he replied. "Used to be an actress in a popular vid series before the war."

Rika had only been a child before the war had started, but had watched a lot of old vids in the years since. She didn't recognize the detective, but a quick check over the Link revealed a long list of performances.

"Well then, this should be entertaining."

The commandant nodded his agreement, and Rika turned her attention back to Kora, who had folded her hands behind her head and appeared to be half asleep.

This continued for almost ten minutes, until finally Caleb slammed his hands down on the table and all but yelled, "You just here for a nap or something?"

To her credit, Kora didn't even flinch. She simply cracked one eye open and gave the man a disinterested look. "I was giving it a shot. Simmer down, I was having a good dream."

"Isn't someone going to come talk to me? Rika, maybe? They brought me up to her ship, after all."

"And what a fucking pain in the ass that was," Kora grumbled. "They're all worried about you getting iced by someone down on the planet, so they haul you up here. But the Marauders are so busy with the mess you made that I get yanked up here from my precinct just to watch you. Fucking annoying."

Caleb didn't respond for a moment, and Rika could see that he was trying to decide what to make of Kora. He had to suspect that she was playing him, but she didn't appear to be in any rush at all, and given the severity of the attacks, that was hard to swallow—it was certainly chafing Rika's nerves.

"Seriously?" the man sat up straight. "They've pulled local cops up to this ship?"

"Yuh huh," Kora replied, closing her eyes again and shifting to get more comfortable. "A few of us. I'm just on first shift. Honestly, I'm pretty happy to be up here. Things are a total shitstorm down on Belgium."

"And you're not going to question me?"

Kora opened her eyes again and fixed Caleb with a withering stare. "Look, buddy. I'm looking at this as a silver lining. I don't have to interview a thousand people about what they saw, or pore through vidstreams looking for clues. All I have to do is make sure that an asswipe like you doesn't get offed. And honestly, I can do that with both eyes closed."

"No you can't," Caleb hissed. "There are people out there who will see me dead before I can talk. I know they have people in the police departments. If they brought cops up here, then it's only a matter of time before someone comes in here shooting."

"Think so?" Her tone was disinterested. "Think some cop from down in Jague would start shooting on a ship loaded with mechs? That'd be suicide."

"People can be motivated to do suicidal things," he countered.

"What if it was me who was sent here to kill you," Kora asked, "and I'm just biding my time?"

"That thought had crossed my mind."

<*Seems risky,*> Rika said to Niki. <*She'd been building rapport…suggesting she's a threat is going to diminish it for sure.*>

<*Maybe. She does need to address that issue, though. Head-on is best.*>

"Well," Kora shrugged. "If I had been sent to kill you, you'd already be dead. But I wasn't, so you're safe for now."

Caleb snorted. "Nice bluster."

The detective shrugged. "I have a gun, you're defenseless. Sure, the mechs would grind me into hamburger afterward, but you'd still be dead."

"Now that would be a waste of a beautiful woman."

"Tell me about it!" Kora nodded vigorously. "I just got done with a rejuv treatment, too! Not gonna waste that and my life just to ice a dumbass like you."

Caleb shook his head. "I'm starting to realize why they sent you in here."

"Oh? Do tell, I'm curious to know, myself."

"You're really good at this. You're trying to goad me into spilling why I'd be worth taking out."

Kora closed her eyes and leant her head back once more. "Spill, don't spill, I don't care. I got sent up here because I'm an asshole. I don't have friends or family, no one likes me, so there's no one I care about. I'm unblackmailable, and I'm self-centered. That means no one can coerce me into killing you. However, I'm not supposed to interrogate you *because* I'm such an asshole, which means they think I'm useless for anything other than guard duty, which means I'm taking a core-damned nap. That is if you'd shut the fuck up for a minute or two."

"Damn," Rika muttered, glancing at Commandant Perin. "I'm starting to believe her."

"One of Kora's many skills," he replied. "She almost has him."

Caleb shook his head as he stared incredulously at Kora. "I can totally believe that. You're one hell of an unlikable person."

"And you need to believe that you should shut the fuck up," Kora shot back. "What part of 'I want to nap' don't you understand? Seriously. You should catch some Zs too. You're gonna get put through the wringer soon enough. I can have them dim the lights if you'd like."

"The wringer?" Caleb asked. "Do you know what they have in mind?"

Kora cracked an eye and looked him up and down. Then she opened both and looked around the room. "I really shouldn't say. They're probably listening."

"You can't disable the monitoring?"

She snorted. "If this were a room back in my station, sure. But we're on a mech ship. They call the shots here."

"Can you give me a hint?" Caleb implored. "Just something to give me an idea."

"Wellll…from what I hear, they have the ability to make new mechs, and since there's a dwindling supply of their people…."

"No!" Caleb's mouth hung open. "They'd turn me into…a fucking *thing*?"

The detective shook her head. "That probably wasn't the wisest thing to say, what with them listening and all."

"Shit," he shook his head, glancing around. "Shit shit shit shit shit!"

Kora chuckled and shook her head. "I'll give you a heads up when they're on their way to get you. Till then, you should try to relax. Meditate or something. Heck, you're not locked down. Get up and do some yoga. Ha, I bet you'll make a great mech. I wonder if they still use Discipline on new recruits like you."

"Look, I'll tell you who hired me." The words tumbled out of Caleb's mouth almost too fast to understand. "I always planned to spill it, I just wanted to play the game, you know? See what I could manage to get out of the deal."

"Whatever," Kora shrugged. "I can't offer you any deals. I'm just a glorified babysitter."

"Hey!" Caleb shouted at the wall behind Kora. "I know you're watching me! I can give you everything, all my contacts! Just don't turn—"

Kora snorted. "You should be really careful what you say next. Plus, you should probably give them a name, something to start on, otherwise they're gonna start on you."

"OK." Caleb nodded. "I didn't talk to the guy at the top, but his name was Xa."

<Nice work, Kora,> Rika said. *<From the intel we have, Xa is a name that has come up in reference to the Nietzschean spy network. I guess it's safe to assume they're not just going to let the death of their emperor go.>*

<Happy to help,> the detective replied. *<I'll keep him going for a bit, see what else he'll volunteer before we get down to brass tacks.>*

<Excellent. I'm going to pass this on to the folks on the ground and attend to a few other crises. Keep up the good work.> She turned to the commandant. "More than glad you two came up here today. Reach out to me if you need anything, or feel free to contact Piper, the ship's AI."

"Of course, Colonel Rika," the commandant said. "I'll also send a request down to my people to look for anything they have on Xa and pass it along."

<Let's not do that quite yet,> Niki cautioned. *<If there are in fact people in your department that the Niets have in their pocket—which isn't that far-fetched—then we don't want to make it known that we're looking for Xa.>*

The commandant's face took on a pained expression, but he nodded in agreement. "OK, I can accept that. We *were* occupied for a long time…loyalties are muddy at best."

"Good," Rika nodded. "I trust you two to keep this under wraps."

<You don't really trust them, do you?> Niki asked her privately. *<This could all be a ruse.>*

<Trust but verify,> Rika intoned. *<Have Piper watch their communications like a hawk.>*

<You say that as though both he and I haven't already cracked

their point-to-point encryption.>

MAGNUS

STELLAR DATE: 05.26.8950 (Adjusted Years)
LOCATION: *Fury Lance*, Belgium
REGION: Genevia System, New Genevian Alliance

"OK, David, what do you have for me?" Rika asked as she strode into the conference room where the P-Cog waited.

The man was seated at the far side of the table, the cooling fins atop his head glinting in the light. He rose and saluted before responding.

"Not just me, ma'am. Niki and Piper were huge helps. It was a team effort."

<Don't listen to him,> Piper chimed in. *<For a man with such a tiny brain, he can ferret out details that even I omit.>*

Rika chuckled at the AI's comment. It was well known in the Marauders that David's brain was a formidable weapon. He'd been instrumental in both avoiding and winning a number of conflicts.

Like the mechs, he'd been modified by the former Genevian military during the war. In his case, they'd identified his impressive mental capabilities, and enhanced them with a variety of augmentations that required additional cooling—hence what people referred to as the 'shark fins' on his head.

When the ISF had upgraded the mechs to Mark 4 models, they'd offered to improve the conditions for David and the other Marauders who had been heavily modded during the war.

While P-Cogs like David had taken upgrades related to function and comfort, they'd all retained their cranial cooling fins. They didn't really need them anymore, but the general consensus was that if the mechs still had bolt-on limbs, P-Cogs and other personnel could show support with their hardware.

Rika sat, and David followed suit before activating the holodisplay.

"Of course, the issue we've been dealing with is who owns what in the battalion. The arrangement you worked out with General Mill stipulated that all mechs own themselves, free and clear. I've put together a mountain of documentation to back this up, and there's no way anyone could claim that the Marauders organization has any claim to the mechs or any hardware that is a part of your standard loadouts."

"I feel a 'but' coming," Rika muttered.

<*There are a lot of buts,*> Niki added.

"A sea of buts." David gave a rueful laugh. "OK, so here's where it's tricky. Not everyone's contract was done up at the same time, or by the same teams. A 'standard loadout' varies a lot, and the Mark 4 upgrades the ISF gave you—as part of a contract with the Marauders—muddy that further. We've found a fair bit of verbiage that makes it flexible, and I've crafted a document that states that 'standard' is any loadout used in multiple engagements—on a mech-by-mech basis."

"OK." Rika nodded, waiting for the other shoe to drop. "Seems reasonable."

"Yeah, so far, so good," the P-Cog replied. "The AIs are all free and clear as well, of course. They own themselves and all their hardware. It's the ships and the employment contracts that are the sticking points. I've looked for loopholes in this, but it's iron-clad. The ships are all the property of the Marauder organization. Hull, engines, and hab. Not only that, but if you resign your commission, you're required to turn all company equipment over to the next-highest ranking senior officer in your command. If none such are present, you're responsible for delivering them to a Marauder officer of flag rank."

"Right." Rika felt a sense of growing frustration. "I know all this."

David nodded. "Sorry, I'm just establishing what we know to be fact, versus what we've been able to rule out as a non-issue, or something we can work around. But I restate this to explain a bitty bit of wiggle room I found buried deep in the regs."

"Oh? Sounds like a loophole." Rika straightened. "I like loopholes."

"Yeah, I think this qualifies as such," David said. "Marauder ships and assets can be delivered to a flag officer of a multi-star alliance with which the Marauders have a Type-9A through 11C contract."

"Shit…" Rika shook her head in wonder. "And we just so happen to have a flag officer of a multi-star alliance with which the Marauders have a Type 11A contract. So I just need to resign my commission and then hand the ships over to Admiral Carson?"

<*Well….*> Niki drew the word out. <*There are a few more steps than that.*>

"Right," David pulled up the regulation on the holodisplay. "You can see that this particular element of the regs is not in newer contracts, just a smattering of older ones. The version of the regs you signed, Rika, doesn't allow for this."

"Of course not," she muttered. "That'd be too easy."

"In fact, of the Marauders currently present in Genevia, only one has signed a contract linked to this version of the regs—a Marauder who has stubbornly refused to sign new versions of the company regs for one reason or another."

The date of the regs and the words 'stubbornly refused' cemented who that single Marauder would be.

"Barne."

<*Told you she'd figure it out,*> Niki said.

"But Barne's not an officer," Rika pointed out. "And he'd have to be a colonel to match the rank requirements to take over the fleet and then turn it over to Carson."

<*We're getting there.*> Piper chuckled. <*Trust me, this is just the beginning.*>

"Let's skip over Barne as a colonel for a moment." David winked as he spoke. "Which is hard, I know, but I want to explain fully what that gets us."

"I'm all ears," Rika replied.

"OK, so, the Scipio Alliance, of which the ISF is a member, has a stipulation that flag admirals can assign member state resources for use by other member states, should both parties be willing. Legally, *you* can't be 'willing', but our hypothetical Colonel Barne could be."

"And the Marauders qualify as a member state?" Rika asked.

"Soooort of," David wobbled his hand back and forth. "Technically, the Marauders signed on to the Scipio Alliance via their contracts with Septhia and Thebes, both of which signed onto Scipio. Almost all Marauders are citizens of those two nations, and thus subject to the Alliance."

Rika couldn't help but laugh at what was, in essence, a simple solution. "So basically, the Marauders are part of the Scipio Alliance by dint of all the leadership being citizens of nations that are part of the alliance. And Admiral Carson has the authority to transfer assets between nation states, so long as the states are willing."

"Even if they're not, in some cases," David added. "Not that we need to enumerate those right now. The problem, of course, is that there's no member state for him to transfer the assets *to*."

"Does he have to transfer?" Rika asked. "Can't he co-opt the assets and then place them under his command? Carson's good people. I wouldn't mind having him as my CO."

Niki sighed. <*That would be too easy. If that were the case, we could have him directly take control from you and then hand it back to you under his direction. There'd be some legal hoops to jump through to get all the contracts right, but if it were possible, it would make your battalion into an autonomous arm of the ISF.*>

Rika snorted. " 'Autonomous arm' that makes us sounds strangely disembodied."

<*I just sighed, do I need to do it again?*>

"Uh…no."

"But someone back at Scipio forced this little clause into the Alliance's founding documents," David continued, giving Rika a bemused glance. "They state that the ISF cannot transfer assets to itself. I guess they were paranoid that Tangel would just seize everything willy-nilly."

"Damn!" Rika shook her head. "I think I see where this is going."

"Right. There needs to be a member state that Carson can transfer to, and there needs to be someone running that member state that you can trust, Rika."

<*And that your Marauders will allow themselves to be entrusted to,*> Piper added. <*And I count myself amongst that number.*>

"OK," Rika held up her hands. "Let me walk through all of this. First, Barne needs to become a full-bird colonel…somehow. Then I need to resign my commission and transfer command to him. Following that, I have to become high-muckity-muck of Genevia, and then join the Scipio Alliance, and then have Carson pass command of the Marauders over to me."

David nodded. "In a nutshell, yeah."

"I have to put it out there—what if I just hop through a jump gate back to the Ontario System and tell General Julia that New Genevia is going to buy my battalion's equipment? Or hell, we just send it all back. We captured a ton of ships, we can just swap all our ISF upgrades to them and send the Marauder ships back."

"Well..." David stroked his chin. "Teeechnically, if you send the ships back, you have to go with them. But I can see that being let slide. So long as we could confirm delivery. But keep in mind that's a *huge* undertaking. It would take months to swap all the ISF shields and weaponry to new ships, then put jump gate mirrors on the ships we're sending back, then send them, remove the mirrors, and jump back."

<*Not to mention you'd have to tell Heather that she's losing the* Fury Lance,> Niki added.

"I'd have to tell that to myself, too," Rika muttered. "Keeping the *Lance* is important. It's our heart."

"Not exactly how we see it, ma'am," David gave her a knowing look. "Regarding going back to Ontario to get dispensation from General Julia, that's an option, but we're not sure she's there. When the ISF lost their QuanComm Network up at Khardine, the Ontario System was cut off. The Septhian president has a functional connection to the galactic network, but he's not at Ontario right now."

"Gah!" Rika leant back in her chair and ran a hand through her hair. "All this just to stay within the letter of the law. Makes a girl wish she wasn't so strait-laced."

<*A strait-laced girl?*> Niki asked with a laugh. <*Where?*>

"What's with all the attempts at humor, lately?"

"Doing this the right way is important." David's voice was calm and level. "At some point, the rest of the Marauders are going to come home. There's a chance that the brass is going to want a seat at the table, and if they can claim you stole your fleet—or that you were operating under them the whole time because you never properly relinquished your command—you'll be giving them leverage to control you."

"See, Niki?" Rika asked. "I *am* strait-laced. A tyrant would just off them if they tried to pull that shit, but here I am, jumping through hoops to avoid a political fight, years in the future."

"Or it could be on our doorstep in a few short months," David said. "We're only a six months' journey from Ontario."

"OK," Rika squared her shoulders. "So we'll do all that. But how do we make Barne a colonel and then transfer the command to him?"

"We're still working on that," the P-Cog said. "I'm still chasing down some options. One of them is for you and Lieutenant Colonel Heather to be dead, or incapacitated, but that's not ideal. I'm running through simulated legal battles if you were to be out of the system for an extended period of time. It's possible at that point that a master sergeant could assume the rank of a colonel to effect command of a fleet."

"Sounds messy," Rika replied.

<Really messy,> Piper said. *<I'm more interested in sorting out how we make you queen.>*

"Acting president," Rika corrected, shaking her head in mock dismay. "I should have more actively quashed that queen nonsense when I had a chance."

<Well, that chance is past.>

"OK, so, how do I legally go about becoming acting president?" Rika asked.

"You know," David mused. "You'd think that with the millions of nations that have been established over the years, there'd be a playbook for this sort of thing, but there's not—or at least, not one that I'm aware of."

"Can we just reconvene the prior government in some fashion?" Rika asked.

"Sure," the P-Cog nodded. "Not only can we, but there's precedent. There was a civil war a few hundred years back, and the government was forced out, but eventually re-took Genevia and then reconvened. Since we have the former president, we could pull that off."

"Except our president doesn't want to be president."

David pursed his lips. "Right."

"Sooooo..."

"Well...." He paused, giving Rika an apologetic look. "You know how the Genevian Alliance evolved out of the old Kunta Triumvirate, of course."

"I do," Rika replied. "And before that, the Asmovians."

"Yes, exactly. Well, when new nations emerge, sometimes a lot of vestiges of the past come along with them. Er...let me take a step back. Something that's easy to forget about Kunta is that they were called a triumvirate, but in their later years, they were ruled by just one person: a magnus."

A disconcerting feeling started up in Rika's stomach, but she signaled for the P-Cog to continue.

"Well, when the democrats won out and the triumvirate was laid to rest, they didn't exactly throw out the old laws, they just said that a democratically elected president overruled a magnus."

<*That's a gross oversimplification,*> Piper interjected.

"Well, yeah, but we don't have all day," David replied. "Either way, the Genevian Constitution still supports the role of magnus."

"What's the criteria to become magnus?" Rika asked, wondering how she'd feel about the title. Somehow it felt even more pretentious than 'queen'.

"Shockingly, it's pretty simple. You just have to command the dominant Genevian military in the system and be Genevian."

"Well, crap..." Rika muttered. "The Marauders aren't a Genevian military, legally speaking. We're mercenaries officially operating out of other nations."

<*It does make things difficult,*> Piper said. <*We need to make a*

Genevian military, and then put you in command of it.>

"Once we sort out how to make Barne a colonel," Rika added.

PICKING PIECES

STELLAR DATE: 05.27.8950 (Adjusted Years)
LOCATION: City of Jague, Belgium
REGION: Genevia System, New Genevian Alliance

Leslie climbed through the wreckage inside the Pandora Tower, making her way to the location the inspection team had flagged.

She'd spent most of her time around the support struts that had been destroyed, but one of the inspectors had found evidence in debris halfway across the building that she hoped would finally provide a clue.

Caleb had told her that he did not set the bomb on the alternate route. He'd said the same to Jague's detectives up on the *Lance,* so Leslie was inclined to believe him—especially because his antimatter bomb would have taken out the alternate route as well as the primary.

She took a moment to consider that Pandora Tower wouldn't just have been damaged and held up by a-grav columns, but completely vaporized. That led her to thinking about how close they'd come to being killed the day before. Not just a few Marauders in an engagement—which was something they always held in mind—but all of M Company would have died in the blast. It would have been devastating.

Barne had left with Caleb not long after Rika returned to the *Fury Lance,* but he'd reached out to Leslie several times to make sure she was alright. It was uncharacteristic for him, and a little unnerving to boot, but she understood the impetus.

Walking through the tower was a surreal experience. The hall she was moving through appeared undamaged, other than a thin crack running along one wall.

The next corridor, however, was all but shredded.

Ejecta from the explosions had careened through the area, blasting holes in the walls for over sixty meters. It was to the end of one of the paths of destruction that the inspectors' marker led her.

Three men and a woman stood around a chunk of carbon-plas column that was wedged between the ceiling and some poor person's desk.

Lieutenant Kirk, the chief bomb inspector for the city of Jague, gave her a sober nod as she approached. "Captain Leslie, I think we finally have some real evidence."

"About time, too," one of the other men said. "So far, all we've found was a bit of residue from the initial explosion."

"I'll be glad to put this mystery to bed," she replied. "As I'm sure will all of you."

Her words were met with solemn nods. Buildings like the Pandora Tower *should* be very hard to bring down. Being a kilometer tall, they were designed to handle incredible wind forces, earthquakes, and even low-yield nuclear explosions.

The tower was supported by six main struts arranged in a hexagon, with cross connections stretched between them at regular intervals. It was designed to flex and move, but still remain rigid enough to halt movement long before it reached a collapse point. The structure was designed to survive losing three of the struts, so long as all three weren't adjacent—which is exactly what had happened in the explosion. Even so, there were backup a-grav generators that should have held the tower up, but they had been destroyed as well.

It annoyed Leslie to no end that someone could have coordinated such a well-planned and executed operation, and no one had spotted anything out of the ordinary.

The issue that had thus far stumped the investigatory team was that the amount of force required to shred a carbon-plas support column was immense. Enough that the blast should have torn apart half the building, flinging it in all directions.

Instead, it had done exactly what was needed to drop the tower directly on the Marauders moving past.

Kirk pointed at the end of the strut that had plowed halfway through the desk before getting stuck. It was clear that it had suffered catastrophic superheating where the material had moved from solid to gas without first passing through the liquid stage. Twists and bubbles were present all along the surface, but there were also cracks running up the column.

"These cracks point to an explosive source *inside* the strut," he explained. "I've also sent microprobes in, and they confirm that the locations where the material endured the highest temperatures are in the core."

"So you're telling me that they got the explosive into the middle of the strut?"

Leslie knew she was repeating his words, but she couldn't help but feel the need to confirm them, given how unlikely such a thing was.

Kirk gave her an understanding look. "Trust me, we checked and re-checked that before we called you. But what we found in that re-checking explained it all."

"Oh?"

"There are signs of an *intense* gamma burst…it radiates out from the inside of the column as well."

Leslie shook her head, knowing that another chat with Caleb was in order. Only antimatter could cause such a large blast.

"I want the ISF team to come and take samples," she said. "They might be able to determine if it's the same antimatter the other bomb used."

"Not sure how they could do that," Kirk said, shaking his head.

"They might not be able to, but if we can confirm or rule

out whether this material came from the same source, it would help the investigation immensely."

"I understand," Kirk replied.

Leslie clapped a hand on his shoulder. "Good work. Really good work. We're going to figure out who did this, and ensure they are brought to justice."

"So long as justice is a death penalty," one of the investigators muttered.

Not acknowledging the statement, Leslie bid her farewells and walked back the way she'd come, and then out of the building. Two massive a-grav pillars stood on either side of the entrance, supporting the building and freeing up the *Fury Lance* to resume its orbit.

They had been flown in from a construction site on the far side of the planet, where they were to be used to support a dam during repairs. That was on hold now, as ensuring that Pandora Tower didn't come down and take out a half dozen other buildings was paramount.

The air seemed to thrum around the pillars, and Leslie could feel the lightness caused by the negative gravitons pulling the building up, lessening its apparent mass, and keeping it from crashing to the ground.

While feeling the side effects of negative gravitons was a common experience for anyone who flew on starships, it was odd to feel it on the ground, and Leslie moved across the street before reaching out to Rika.

<How're things up there, Colonel?>

<As good as can be expected.> Rika sounded tired. *<I met a detective I want to steal from the local cops, but now probably isn't the best time to do it.>*

Leslie held in a laugh. *<No, probably not. They wouldn't have a lot of warm fuzzies if you did that. I have an update, though.>*

<Oh?> Rika's tone brightened measurably. *<What's new?>*

<Turns out that the only thing that could have taken out Pandora

Tower's struts was antimatter. We found a chunk of one that bears signs matching that hypothesis, so it's our working theory for now.>

<*That seems like more than a coincidence,*> Rika said.

<*Agreed. Though the bombs and methods are very, very different. I'm inclined to believe Caleb when he says that he didn't know about this other bomb.*>

<*I am too, but I'll let Kora know this and see if she can dig anything further out.*>

<*That your new detective friend?*>

<*Yeah,*> Rika laughed softly. <*You really need to watch the interrogation video when you have time. She's something else.*>

<*I'll make a note of it,*> Leslie replied. <*I saw in the report that he gave a name, someone called Xa. Any leads yet?*>

<*No, and it's annoying. Piper is sifting through every database he can lay hands on, but so far, no sign. He's also looking for missing antimatter, but with all the half-destroyed ships floating around, that's like trying to determine if a piece of hay is missing from a haystack.*>

Leslie sighed and leant back against the building behind her. <*Yeah, I can imagine. OK, I'm going to head to the spaceport and throw the mark 1 eyeball on their reports and see if I can dig up a clue. They don't store any antimatter planetside, but there's no way someone could have gotten it down here without it tripping a mag-field detector.*>

<*Or they just didn't bring it down through the spaceport. A thousand ships have touched down wherever they wanted to over the past few weeks.*>

<*Tell me about it. But at least it'll rule something out.*>

<*Agreed,*> Rika replied. <*Well, good luck.*>

Leslie barked a laugh that she passed along over the Link. <*Yeah, I'm gonna need it. This whole sticking around and policing thing sucks, by the way. When do we ship out?*>

<*Funny, Leslie. Real funny.*>

RIKA MAGNUS

STELLAR DATE: 05.28.8950 (Adjusted Years)
LOCATION: *Fury Lance,* Belgium
REGION: Genevia System, New Genevian Alliance

Rika stood before her command team in one of the larger briefing rooms aboard the *Fury Lance*. It was becoming quite the sizable group, with the captains of the new companies and the commanders of captured ships in attendance.

Admiral Carson of the ISF was also present, along with two rear admirals and a general. They were sitting near the back, and a curious smile rested on the admiral's lips.

Not for the first time, Rika wondered what he thought of the mechs and their mission to free Genevia and defeat Nietzschea. Carson had been born over five thousand years prior, in the golden age of the Sol System. He'd flown engagements out in the deep black before the days of FTL, when a ship lost beyond Sol's heliopause may never be seen again. No artificial gravity, no advanced shields, just your hull, mods to handle extreme *g*s, and a total lack of fear. Though he ran his fleet professionally, something about the way the man held himself belied the past crucible that had forged him.

She wondered what had prompted him to take a berth on the ancient colony ship that had taken him from the Sol System—and forward in time. He must have wanted a change of some sort…

Rika found herself curious if he'd gotten more or less than he'd expected.

"OK, people," she said once everyone had settled into place. "We have a plan on how to retain the fleet legally, and for me to take command of New Genevia so that we can settle things down and move on to Nietzschea. Well, by 'plan', I mean strategy. We have some tactical holes that need plugging, so I'm looking for plugs."

Without further preamble, she launched into the plan to take command of the system, transfer the fleet to Barne, and then utilize Admiral Carson to transfer the Marauder assets to Genevia, and thus back to Rika.

"Doesn't that seem a bit shaky, Colonel?" Silva asked after Rika was finished. "I don't mean to disparage all your hard work, but can't someone from Marauder command show up and rescind Barne's acceptance of Admiral Carson's transfer request?"

"Like to see them try," Barne grunted.

"Not so easy," Carson said from his seat in the back. "The wording of the Alliance states that it's for the duration of the war, unless the receiving party turns the assets back over of their own free will. Since the idea here is to maintain a legal claim, that will do. If your brass is dumb enough to try and make a play for your position here, they'll have a difficult time of it."

Heather barked a laugh. "That's one way to put it."

"Still, I want to set things up properly." Rika surveyed her leadership with stern eyes. "The more care we take to have a solid, legal claim for what we're doing here, the less trouble we'll face later on. That's going to make things a lot better for our people. Liberation, and reconstruction afterward, is going to be hard enough as it is without infighting.

"So, with that in mind, who has ideas on our two major hurdles?"

"Just to be clear," Barne dragged the words out. "You're sure that 'fuck 'em' isn't a valid strategy?"

"I'm sure, Master Sergeant," Rika replied, and the man subsided.

"Well..." Captain Vargo Klen spoke up from close to the

back of the room. "I might have a solution for your problem."

Rika cocked an eyebrow. Vargo had a shrouded past, one that he'd only revealed in dribs and drabs. One of the things in his past was that he'd once been the governor of a planet. No one had been able to discern which, and some suspected that he'd been in charge of an entire star system. In proper Marauder style, there were a number of betting pools established for the system, scope, and time of his governorship.

"I'm all ears, Captain," she said.

"Well, as you all know, I was a governor once. That was way, way back. But more recently, I had some other jobs. One of which was in the GAF."

"Right," Silva said, casting the man a suspicious look. "You were a lieutenant, a pilot."

"At one point, yes," the man replied. "But before that, a while before that, I was a general."

An incredulous snort tore its way out of Barne's throat, earning him an elbow from Leslie.

"I know, I know, it's hard to believe," Vargo said. "It was a lifetime before I re-enlisted to be a pilot. I like to keep my pasts separate."

"How many do you have?" Captain Travis asked.

A smile crept across Vargo's lips, and he winked at the other man. "Now that would be telling."

"So, a general," Rika shook her head, speaking the words as a statement. "In the GAF."

"Yes, ma'am."

"You sure you should be calling me that? Shouldn't I be 'sir'-ing you?"

He shrugged. "Not Captain Vargo Klen, no. But if I were to be General Drew Mior, then probably."

"This just seems like another catch-22," David said. "Unless

Drew Mior was still active duty at the end of the war."

"Will MIA work?" Vargo asked.

"Sounds a bit like AWOL," Silva said, giving Vargo a sidelong look.

"You know me," Vargo looked around the room. "I'm not one to abandon anyone. I really was MIA, and not in a way I enjoyed. When I finally made it back to Genevia, so much time had passed that I decided it would be better if I just re-enlisted. I had spent some time behind a flight stick, so I decided to become a pilot."

"And you didn't think your experience as a general would have helped?" Barne asked.

"I did help," Vargo countered. "For starters, I had been a peace-time general. When I got back to Genevia, things had already kicked off with the Niets. I would have been stuck at some supply dump, *if* they let me back in at all. I saw that the space force wasn't doing good by the ground pounders, so I decided that by being a friendly voice in the skies, I could better help active combat units."

<*The records are in the planetside archives,*> Piper chimed in. <*Drew Mior really was a general in the GAF…over a hundred years ago.*>

Chase barked a laugh. "That's some serious MIA."

"You have no idea," Vargo replied with a sorrowful nod. "So, technically, if I understand our situation well enough, I take on my old role, and Admiral Carson transfers all the captured Nietzschean ships to me, that way they're not Marauder property at any point."

"OK, that seems like a good start," Rika said. "What next, General Mior?"

"Core, that brings back memories. OK, so once I'm ensconced as the lord and master of all I survey, I promote Barne in the GAF."

"You what?" Barne asked. "How do you do that?"

"There's actually precedent," Vargo explained. "Command-track NCOs can transfer to officer status in times of crisis by a three-star or above."

"Shit, really?" Travis asked. "You were a three-star? And you still suck that bad at Snark?"

"I was—am—a four-star," Vargo explained. "Anyway, that's not the point. Barne has one of the old Marauder contracts that was a little poorly worded. It says that his rank in the Marauders must at least match his highest rank in the GAF."

"Oh shit," Barne muttered, his eyes flicking side-to-side as he examined his HUD. "It does, but there's no time stipulations or anything."

"Right," Vargo said. "Same as mine, incidentally. We signed at the same time, I didn't look up your contract, Barne."

"So then, you recall Barne to active duty in the GAF and promote him," David mused. "He accepts and then resigns his commission, remaining in the Marauders. Following that, you recall Rika to active status in the GAF, and she resigns her commission, turning the fleet over to Barne, who must turn it over to Carson, because he's not of flag rank."

"That's where I was going with this." A grin settled on Vargo's lips. "Then I promote Rika to three-star general, flag rank in the GAF, and resign my own commission. That puts her in command of all the captured Nietzschean vessels, and she is then a Genevian in command of the largest Genevian fleet in the system, making her magnum opus, or whatever."

"Magnus," David corrected.

"Right. Yeah. Once that's done, Carson transfers the Marauder fleet to the ruler of the Genevian System, and then poof, it's all done."

"You forgot something." The P-Cog turned to face Rika. "You'll need to sign on to the Scipio Alliance before Admiral

Carson can transfer the fleet to you," he reminded her.

Rika realized that she was grinning from ear to ear. "OK, that's a no-brainer. But, David?"

"Yeah?"

"Next time, we bring Vargo in on these things."

"You mean General Mior?" he asked with his own wide grin.

"Mior," Barne muttered. "Now that's one hell of a weird name."

Vargo snorted. "Says the guy who is named after where you store animals."

"OK, boys," Rika raised her hands. "Let's just get this kicked off. It's a lot of steps, and we need to do them all in the correct order."

"Yes," David nodded emphatically. "Timing is going to be very, very important."

* * * * *

After the meeting was over, as the team was filing out, Rika called Leslie to the front of the room.

"Any leads yet?"

"No." Leslie shook her head. "Well, I mean, some, but they were all dead ends. Nothing viable. We've found plenty of people doing bad things, mind you, but none we can connect to the antimatter and Xa."

"A sea of crime out there, is it?" Rika asked.

"Stars, you have no idea. Everyone and their dog is taking advantage of the chaos to smuggle shit on and off Belgium. Some of it is totally blatant, too. Mostly we're just noting who's doing what. The local cops don't have the staff to pursue even a fraction of these crimes."

Rika cocked an eyebrow, wondering why Commandant Perin hadn't brought this up. "Are they understaffed?"

"Oh hell yeah. They were augmented by a Nietzschean garrison before.... Seems like the Niets didn't want the cops to have a sizable force of their own, so they kept them lightly armed, and any time the locals needed the big guns, they had to call in the military."

"Guh." Rika shook her head. "That must have sucked. It's going to take us forever to untangle this. I mean...there are thousands of Niets living on Belgium—maybe as many as a million of them across the system. From what I've heard, most are content to live under Genevian rule, so long as they can continue to operate as they have been."

"That's the question, right?" Leslie sighed. "How *have* they been operating? Most are probably criminals by Genevian law, but then a lot of our people probably did things over the past decade that the Niets would allow, but we do not."

"Yeah, don't remind me. I just signed up to be magnus and lord over this mess."

"We're going to have to change that," Chase said as he approached. "Magnus really doesn't suit you. We'd all gotten used to thinking of you as our queen."

Rika groaned. "Oh not you too."

"Rika," Chase's voice grew serious. "You need to stop doing that."

"Doing what?"

Chase and Leslie shared a look before he replied, "Complaining whenever someone calls you queen or president. It'll become a morale issue before long."

Rika felt like she'd just been punched in the stomach. If there was one thing she prided herself on, it was being there for her people. Her Marauders—or whatever they would end up being called once all the political shenanigans were over—were her top priority.

"What he means," Leslie quickly filled in the silence. "Is

that denying your place of leadership means that no one knows who will be in charge. That makes your people feel like you don't want to take care of them, and that you're leaving them in limbo. They need stability and clear structure. You need to own this. Own it like every bit of it was your idea."

Both Marauders wore deadly serious expressions, and Rika realized that her playful dismissal of taking on a meaningful title was only amusing—or something along those lines—to her. To everyone else, it was annoying and insulting.

<You've been deflecting,> Niki joined in. *<It's understandable, but they're right. It's time to step up.>*

Rika pursed her lips, glancing down at her hands as they clenched and unclenched, then squared her shoulders and looked her intel officer and the captain of M Company in the eyes.

"OK. You're right. I can't joke around…or deflect…any longer. But I agree with you, Chase. 'Queen' is way better than 'magnus'."

"Good," Leslie stifled a yawn. "Now that that's settled, I'm going to go get some shut-eye. It's been three days since I've slept."

"Barne gonna let you?" Chase gave her a knowing look.

"He'd better, or I'll kick his ass right out an airlock."

Rika snorted. "I would pay to see that."

PERIL

STELLAR DATE: 05.28.8950 (Adjusted Years)
LOCATION: *Slyfe*
REGION: Gerra System, Old Genevia, Nietzschean Empire

"Captain Becky."

Becky looked up from her silver and gold coffee mug and sighed. "What is it *now*, Dara?"

"Well, the stationmaster's office just reached out and said that the promotional token you tried to use for the docking tug was expired, so we have to pay the full amount."

"Are you kidding me?" Becky half-rose from her captain's seat. "I'm not paying *full price* for a docking tug. I've *never* paid full price. Get me the stationmaster. I'm gonna give him a piece of my mind."

Dara gave a meek nod from her place at the comm station, and turned back to her console. "Yes, Captain. I'll tell them that."

The woman muttered something under her breath, and Becky slid forward to the edge of her seat. "What was that?"

"I—I was just wondering if you ever get tired of doing this?"

"Doing what?" Becky demanded.

"You know," Dara replied quietly. "Pretending you have valid codes for a discount when you don't, then getting…very persistent until they comp us a tug."

Becky snorted before settling back into her seat and taking a sip of her designer coffee. "Well, if my wife had left me with a large enough credit store for shopping *and* nuisances like this, it wouldn't have to happen. But since they can be manipulated so easily, why not?"

"Umm…I guess. Sure. OK, I have the stationmaster. His

name's Barry."

"I know," Becky waved her hand in dismissal. "He and I have done this dance before."

A holoimage of a man appeared before Becky, and she gave a warm smile.

"Barty! Good to see you. I assume you're going to honor our codes?"

"Captain Becky," the man's brow was pulled down almost over his eyes. "You know that's not possible right now. Not only are those codes ancient, but we have more important things to worry about than you trying to save a buck."

"What do you have to worry about?" Becky pressed. "And don't forget, my wife's company does significant trade with your station."

Barry pursed his lips. "With the Niets pulling out, I have no idea who will be doing what sort of trade—which is why we're not going to play your little game this time."

It took a moment for the words to fully sink in, but when they did, she nearly spat out her coffee. "The whats are doing *what*?"

"Shit, Becky, can you drag your face out of your stellar spice latte long enough to check the feeds?" Barry ground out the words in a tone of pure annoyance that he'd never directed at her before. "The Nietzscheans are leaving the Gerra System. Pulling out. Poof."

She rolled the words around in her mind, trying to make sense of them. After some consideration, she replied, "But they can't."

"Well, you can tell them that," Barry said. "Right after you pay full price for a docking tug."

Becky didn't fully hear what the stationmaster had said. Not that she cared. He wasn't focusing on the right issues. "How are they going to police the system? It's not possible!"

"Fuck," Barry muttered, and the holodisplay changed to

show a closeup view of Gepa, the single habitable planet in the Gerra System. A group of Nietzschean cruisers were closer to the viewpoint, and scrolling text at the bottom of the screen read, 'NIETZSCHEAN SYSTEM COMMAND HAS LEFT THE PLANET'.

Shaking her head in disbelief, Becky took another sip. "No. They must just be moving."

"Core, woman! They're not '*moving*'. This is all anyone has been talking about for a day. Check the feeds, all their ships are pulling away fro—"

The stationmaster's words were cut off by Becky's scream as she pointed at the screen. "What're they doing?! Are they—?"

Words failed her as she watched a dozen missiles streak away from the ships on the display, all headed toward Gepa. None of the planetary defenses fired, and a minute later, nuclear fireballs began to appear on the planet's surface.

"Fuuuuuck," Dara breathed out. "They're going to burn it to ash."

"So," Barry responded, the holodisplay flipping back to show his stern features. "Now you understand? Full price for the tug, or I seize your ship for trespassing."

Becky nodded wordlessly.

"Good." Barry closed the connection, and Becky stared down into her coffee.

"I can't believe they did that. How could they?" she whispered.

Dara shook her head. "I don't know, Captain. But we need to decide where we're going. Because it sure isn't to Gepa anymore."

"We're staying faaaaar away from that place," Becky replied, pulling up system traffic reports.

They confirmed what Barry had told her. Nietzschean

warships were boosting away from every station. She didn't know if it represented all of their ships, but a variety of pundits seemed to think so.

"They're heading for nearby jump points," Dara said. "There's only one available to us."

"Which?" Becky asked, and the other woman highlighted it. "Genevia? No no no! Find something else. Robot mercenaries just took Genevia!"

The display flashed red warnings at three locations around the system, and Dara let out a string of expletives.

"What?" Becky demanded.

"Those are—were—stations," Dara whispered. "Captain, Genevia is our best bet. We don't know—"

"Plot it," Becky ordered in quiet resignation. "The moment the tug releases hold of us, we make for the Genevia jump point. I don't care what's going on there. It *has* to be better than this."

RESPITE

STELLAR DATE: 05.28.8950 (Adjusted Years)
LOCATION: ***Fury Lance,*** **Belgium**
REGION: Genevia System, New Genevian Alliance

Rika rolled off Chase and flopped onto the bed next to him, blowing out a long breath followed by a contented sigh.

"You done over there yet?" Chase asked. "I'm trying to go to sleep."

"What?" Rika squeaked, propping herself up on one arm to see a hint of a smile tugging at his lips. "Oh, you jerk. And here I thought I'd somehow made you nod off."

The hint turned into a grin, and he grabbed her shoulder, pulling her close. "No chance, my queen."

"Sto—"

"Nuh uh!" Chase interrupted her, holding up a finger. "You have to get used to it."

"Yeah, sure, but not here," Rika said in protest.

He lifted his lips to meet hers. "Especially here."

They kissed deeply, matte grey flow armor bodies pressed against one another as they sought comfort and succor in sharing themselves with each other.

"My queen," Chase whispered fiercely as they began anew. "I'll serve you forever."

"Oh?" Rika asked, the question punctuated by a gasp. "Does that mean you'll be my consort?"

He reached around and slapped her ass. "Consort? That's all I rate?"

Rika straightened, fixing him with a glare. "Well, I don't know what the law is about taking a king. Besides, that would totally muddy the chain of coma*aaa*aand…"

His hands had found her breasts—which were properly

sensitive after the ISF had performed her Mark 4 upgrades—his thumbs rolling around the small nubs that marked her nipples.

"Oh Finaeus," she moaned.

Chase made a choking sound. "Sorry, what?"

"Er..." Rika giggled with embarrassment. "I was just thanking Finaeus for his attention to detail when he crafted our new bodies."

Chase laughed and grabbed both her shoulders, pulling her back down again, his lips brushing her ear. "Well, if you're all excited about our upgraded bodies, let's do that thing we were talking about the other day. Just..."

"Hmmm?" Rika moaned the question softly.

"Don't call out Finaeus's name. Now I'm picturing his mug in my head."

Rika slid her hands around his back, lifting him until they were both upright. "You know Finaeus is totally hot, right?"

"Stop already!"

* * * * *

An hour later, the couple lay on the bed, chests heaving, and Rika couldn't help but laugh.

"You're not dozing off *now*, are you?"

"I might pass out," Chase slid his hands behind his head. "But it certainly wouldn't qualify as dozing off."

Rika propped herself up again and stared into his eyes. "Do you think I'll make a good queen? Sorry to come off as needy...I just need a bit of affirmation here."

His eyes had been closed, but they opened wide and stared into hers with a look of utter contentment. "Rika, you've been our queen since the day you took the fight to the Politica and freed our people there. But you're not some preening debutante on a throne, you're a warrior who leads from the front and never asks anything of her people that she won't do herself. That's why I follow you. That's why we all follow you."

He reached up and stroked her cheek before his eyes closed once more.

"Thanks, Chase. I really needed to hear that."

"Great, now can you finally let me go to sleep?"

She gave a mock gasp and pinched his arm. "Oh, now you're in for it!"

LEADER ODA

STELLAR DATE: 06.01.8950 (Adjusted Years)
LOCATION: Mount Genevia, Belgium
REGION: Genevia System, New Genevian Alliance

Rika stood at the window of the audience room on the estate atop Mount Genevia, forcing herself to see it as it was now, and not how it had been when she'd fought Constantine's soldiers and killed the Nietzschean emperor.

"It looks different when it's your throne room, doesn't it?" a voice asked from behind her.

She turned to see Tremon entering the room, his shadow, Yakob, not far behind. The former president's guard exchanged a nod with Kelly, who stood near the entrance, watching over Rika.

Keli and Shoshin were nearby, prowling the halls in full stealth, keeping an eye peeled for anything that could harm their new queen—the only title they used for her now, though it would still be some time before she'd be coronated.

"Is it different now that it's not yours?" Rika asked the man who had once called the estate his home.

Tremon chuckled as he reached her side and looked out over the valley below, something made easier due to the swath of destruction Colonel Borden's Starcrusher had wreaked when it climbed the mountain.

"It was never my throne room, Rika. When I was president, this was a meeting room with a large, circular table, designed to show that the senators who sat there with me were all equal." He paused and gave a soft laugh. "Granted, my chair was bigger than theirs."

"I knew it," Rika said, bumping her hip against Tremon's elbow.

"Damn, Rika, you're like a boulder."

"Sorry, I'm used to doing that with mechs. They barely notice."

"Well, you'll have to get used to being around more of us squishies. We're a lot more fragile."

"Yeah," she sighed. "We're trying not to call you regular people that. Sorry."

Tremon shrugged. "I choose to consider it a term of endearment."

"To be honest, sometimes I wonder why everyone doesn't want to become a mech," Rika mused. "We're clearly superior."

"I think you should be happy that most people don't. Imagine if the entire Nietzschean Empire was comprised of mechanized soldiers and populace."

Rika barked a laugh. "You make a good point. Being superior certainly is handy."

"Speaking of people who think they're superior," Tremon drew the final word out, turning to look into Rika's eyes. "You ready to talk to Oda?"

"Fuck," she muttered. "No. No with a side of nope. That guy makes my skin crawl, and that's not even possible."

"He has a lot of connections," Tremon said. "Which surprises me, because he was a nothing during the war. A minor representative from a nowhere moonlet at the front of the system."

"I wonder how he came to be in charge of The Refuge on Faneuil?" Rika mused.

"Probably fled there before anyone else. For all I know, he set up shop there long before the final surrender."

"Fits."

<Speaking of 'he', he's on the lift now,> Niki said. *<So it would probably be best if you didn't both look like you just sucked on a*

lemon.>

Rika pulled a feed from the lift and saw Oda with three other people. Two of the lift's passengers had the appearance and stance of guards, while the third, a woman, stood shoulder to shoulder with Oda.

Rika reviewed the faces she'd seen in Oda's council chamber deep in The Refuge several weeks back, but none were a match.

"Dammit." Tremon shook his head, a look of disgust on his face. "That's Arla. I wonder what rock she was hiding under."

The name didn't mean anything to Rika, but she'd not followed politics in the least during the war. Her momentary look of confusion must have broadcast this to Tremon, because he quickly filled her in.

"She was the minister of finance in the latter half of the war. Due to the way the constitution was set up, she had nearly as much power as the war department itself. I'm honestly shocked she's still alive."

"What do you think she'll want?" Rika asked.

"Control." The word fell from Tremon's lips like a stone. "That is a woman who craves power."

Rika examined the pinched features of the auburn-haired woman. She seemed calm and serene, clean, and in good health. If she'd been somewhere in the system, and not with Oda, she must have been out in the open.

<Niki, she had to have been active somehow in the past ten years. Especially if she is power-hungry like Tremon says. No way she just simpered silently somewhere.>

The AI laughed. *<Nice alliteration. And I'm with you one hundred percent. I'm already digging, trying to figure out where she met up with Oda. If nothing jumps out, we'll have to assume that she was at The Refuge.>*

<She could have gone there recently,> Rika suggested. *<No reason to think she was hiding in the shadows while we were*

visiting.>

<*Keeping aaaall the options open.*>

Rika could feel a slight hum of activity in her mind as Niki began to dig into Arla's origins. The ability to tell when her AI was hard at work wasn't new, but it felt more intense than it had in the past.

A minute later, the visitors were being led into the room by Shoshin. He gestured for the two guards to take up a position on the far side of the room from Kelly—who had shifted so that her gun arm was nearly in a position to fire on them—while he followed Oda and Arla as they walked toward Rika and Tremon.

"Colonel Rika," Oda called out while he was still several meters away. "It is so very nice to see you again."

<*Why does it feel like he's greeting me in his place of residence,*> Rika asked Niki.

<*Because he's an asshat. Love how he made sure to call you 'colonel' too.*>

<*Well, it* **is** *my rank and only current title.*>

<*He's still an asshat.*>

"Welcome to Mount Genevia and the Royal Estate," Rika replied, not feeling above getting her own dig in.

<*Zing!*> came Niki's accompanying comment.

"Royal?" Arla asked. "That seems like a bit of a leap, doesn't it?"

"Rika." She extended her hand. "I don't believe we've ever met, but Tremon has told me all about you."

Arla closed the distance between herself and Rika, clasping hands, though her eyes never met Rika's. "Tremon? Oh! You mean former President Kalvin."

Tremon nodded and extended his hand to Arla once she'd unclasped Rika's.

She took it and gave three firm pumps. "An interesting

change. What precipitated it?"

"Shame," Tremon answered without elaboration before pulling his hand free and offering it to Oda.

Rika followed suit, and then gestured to the arrangement of sofas on her left. "Let's sit and discuss...whatever it is you came here to discuss."

The group moved wordlessly to the couches and settled into them; Rika and Tremon sitting on one, Oda choosing a chair, and Arla taking a seat at the end of a sofa directly across from Rika.

"What we came here to discuss," Oda began after a few moments of contemplative silence, "is how the new government will be structured, and when things will be well-established enough for it to move from Faneuil to Belgium."

"Why would a local planetary government move here?" Rika asked. "Are your people seeking asylum or refuge?"

A look of confusion crossed Oda's face. "Excuse me?"

"So far as I can tell, Leader Oda, you are the governor of one of the minor planets in the Genevia System. As such, you can send a representative to the system's assembly when it is re-formed. The system's assembly can then send a representative to the federal assembly, at such time as one of *those* is re-formed."

"Is this all related to those ridiculous claims people are making that you're a queen now?" Arla asked, her derisive tone matching her expression.

"I think it's just because it's odd to have a colonel in charge," Rika explained. "So they're picking something more powerful."

Arla arched a brow. "But 'queen'?"

"Has a certain ring to it, don't you think?" Tremon's face split into a grin. "And we're in no place to have Genevia-wide elections."

Oda's customary grimace deepened. "For all intents and

purposes, this *is* Genevia."

"I think the people of Blue Ridge, Iberia, and by this point, Parsons, would all disagree with that. They were liberated before Genevia, so why would they have no voice in this?"

Arla and Oda shared a look before Arla spoke. "Because this is the capital."

"The capital of what?" Rika asked. "The only reason Genevia was freed before a host of other systems was because the Nietzschean emperor was here. And he was here because of the Capeton shipyards. None of this had anything to do with Genevia being inherently special—politically speaking, that is."

<*You know that's not true,*> Niki admonished.

<*I do, but I'm not going to cede that point without a fight. It's not instant leverage they get to use against us.*>

"Surely you can't be serious," Arla said, rising to the bait. "There is huge significance to freeing the Genevia System. I can't believe that someone who has made it as far as you wouldn't be able to see that."

"I see that it's a big symbol to you," Rika replied. "But I grew up far from here, was enslaved by people who ruled from here, and then was their slave in a war that they botched and lost."

Tremon looked uncomfortable at Rika's words, and she wished that they didn't include him in their accusations, but they did. There was nothing either of them could do about that part of their respective pasts.

"I wouldn't say we botched—" Arla began, but Rika interrupted her.

"Are you going to look at what my Marauders have done in the past year and tell me that the GAF used us properly during the war? Because I'll tell you this, if *I* had been in command, we would never have lost. Genevia would have defeated Nietzschea, without a doubt."

A look of innocence settled on Oda's face. "The man responsible for all of that sits beside you."

Rika shrugged. "He apologized, and I believe him."

"And yet you blame us." Oda spoke the words as a statement, not a question.

"I think that's your guilt speaking." Rika fixed him with a steely-eyed stare. "What I was getting at was not that I have a list of people to blame, but that Genevia holds no special place in my heart."

A scowl settled on Arla's brow. "Well, you're going to have to forgive *us* for being a bit nervous talking to a woman who is carrying enough weaponry to kill us a dozen times over."

Rika laughed. "That must be a part of why we lost the war—you don't have the most basic understanding of a mech's abilities. My weapons could kill you a thousand times over."

<*That probably didn't help,*> Niki commented.

<*No, but it sure made me feel better. Any word on where Arla's been hiding?*>

<*Still working on it.*>

"OK," Tremon's tone was mollifying. "None of us are here to do harm to the others, but let's set aside that talk."

"Fine." Oda nodded. "Then we can discuss the interim government that will take care of Genevia until such time as we can hold elections."

"I'll listen to your thoughts," Rika replied with a casual swipe of her hand. "But we already have our own plans in motion."

As Oda launched into a spiel about how he and Arla were uniquely qualified to manage Genevia's affairs, Rika reached out to Leslie.

<*I feel like things will come to a head today. Where are we on Oda's messages?*>

<Piper and I are certain that we have the location of the trigger device, my liege.>

<You're so funny,> Rika drawled. *<I'm going to put a filter on our conversations to change words I don't like.>*

<Oh where's the fun in that?> Leslie complained. *<I'm working up quite the lexicon. I'll be the most well-versed lady of your court in all the proper manners, pomp, and ceremony.>*

<Sure,> Rika sent a derisive sound along with the word. *<I'd actually pay good credit to see you do pomp and ceremony. Oh core. He's talking about changes to the currency now. We just finished establishing a system-wide bank to stabilize the economy. Where's he been?>*

<He's ignoring what you've done to undermine you.>

<I'm going to undermine him right out the window,> Rika grunted. *<I should probably pay attention again. Keep me posted.>*

<Will do, Your Highness.>

* * * * *

"OK," Leslie addressed her team after closing the connection with Rika. "Our baddies are in here somewhere. They've got the signal trigger, so we just have to find them, disable it, and then we can go for hot dogs."

"Wait, Captain," Kor held up a hand. "Why hot dogs? I like burgers."

Leslie shrugged. "It just sounded good. You can have a burger if you want."

"Awesome, I—"

"Kor, would you shut up," Sergeant Alison grunted. "Just cover Jenisa's six, or I'll make you eat your own hot dog."

He cocked his head, and Leslie knew he was grinning. "I'd rather have Fred's hot dog."

Fred slapped away Kor's outstretched hand. "You touch

my hot dog, and I'll cut off your hand and swap it out for a toaster."

"I'd rather have a pot for boiling hot dogs."

"Wait," Jenisa shook her head. "I thought you preferred burgers?"

"Damn, I do."

Jenisa clapped a hand on his shoulder. "And now you're gonna eat Fred's dick."

"Like hell he is."

"People," Alison hissed. "Can we *focus*?"

"I'd just like to say," Randy chimed in, "that I'm a vegetarian. But Fred's hot dog doesn't have any meat, so I think I could eat it in a pinch."

"Maybe a corndog," Kor mused.

Alison took a step toward him, and he backed away.

"OK, OK. Sorry, Sarge. Just having a little fun."

"Yeah, well, go have fun on the route I assigned you. Wait…no. No fun. None of you have any fun. Just do your damn jobs."

The four mechs in the fireteam split up, moving out of the small loading bay and into the building beyond. Kor was still laughing softly, and Leslie couldn't help smiling along with him.

"I love working with your team, Alison. I'm really glad you didn't all die back at Iberia."

"Uhh…thanks? I think?"

"Kidding, Alison. Well, about joking about you dying. Not about working with your team."

The sound of a low sigh came from the SMI-4. "Well, someone has to."

"The words of someone who needs a vacation, I think."

"What?" Alison lifted a hand to her shoulder and checked a charge cylinder pouch. "I suppose, maybe. It's just hard being in Genevia—especially on Belgium."

"Is it?" Leslie asked. "Why?"

"It's where I was mechanized," the SMI-4 said with a shrug. "It's nuts. I've walked battlefields where comrades have fallen, and not been as fazed as I am just sharing a planet with the facility that turned me into a mech."

"OK...that is a bit odd." Leslie's tail whipped from side to side as she considered the rationale behind the sergeant's statement.

"Sheesh, Captain, I was looking for support."

"Oh! Sorry, at first, I thought this was the 'here be the crucible that forged me' speech. I'm still catching up."

Alison snorted. "Barne's wearing off on you."

"Hey," Leslie growled. "That's not the sort of thing you say to your CO."

"You're not my CO. Captain Chase is."

"Yeah, well, I used to be, so don't forget it."

Neither woman spoke for several minutes, watching the feeds on their HUDs, which showed the two teams moving around the perimeter of the building's first floor while drones began to sweep through the interior.

It was most likely that their target was on an upper floor, but they needed to ensure that each level was clear—or at least flag any enemies—before climbing to the next.

In all honesty, the mission wasn't that important in Leslie's eyes. Worst-case scenario, a broadcast would go out informing the system that Oda was the leader of Genevia, and Rika would counter that with a simple message that Belgium was the capital and to continue to direct requests through her.

It would have been nice if they'd already been able to perform the complex dance that David, Niki, and Piper had worked out, but it was still in progress—though by day's end, Vargo Klen should be in command of a host of ships that had been captured in the battle or taken from the shipyards. Once that happened, a smooth progression of events would lead to Rika's inevitable assumption of power.

"What do you think Rika really makes of all this?" Alison asked.

"You reading my thoughts?"

"I suspect it's what every Marauder is thinking already. We all want to keep Rika as our old lady. Being queen suits her, so long as she gets to remain the warrior as well."

Leslie remembered the first time she'd laid eyes on Rika. The woman had been shipped to Berlin in a cryo tube, and it had been up to the members of Team Basilisk to reassemble her, which they had, only to learn that she'd been purchased at auction.

Leslie had never told Rika, but when the woman's blue eyes had first snapped open in that cryo tube, they'd been filled with fear, loathing, and regret. These had been replaced with anger and a fire that only Rika possessed, but one that had lessened over time.

Even her personal growth is inspiring.

"I guess you're right," she finally replied to the SMI-4. "Rika's our warrior queen. Accept no substitute."

<*You two seeing this?*> Jenisa asked a moment later.

Leslie tapped the private's feed and saw that she'd come upon a makeshift comm array near the northeast corner of the building.

<*And here I thought it would be on the roof,*> Leslie said. <*But it looks like the antenna is right there.*>

<*It's kinda big, though,*> Jenisa said. <*Why's it so big?*>

<*Piper?*> Leslie reached out to the AI. <*I hate to always be pestering you, but we have a bit of a curiosity here.*>

<*Leslie, you were instrumental in freeing me from eternal slavery. I will always answer your call.*>

<*You have a thing for me?*> she asked with a laugh. <*Wait, no, don't answer that. Barne would* ***not*** *go there.*>

<*You had a question?*> the AI asked.

Leslie sent him a feed of the comm array, while Alison asked, <*Why is it unprotected?*>

An explosion rocked the building, and Leslie swore as the two rushed inside.

<*You just had to say that.*>

* * * * *

"…so you see, that's why we need to restructure the military complex to support that type of defense buildup." Arla spoke the words slowly, as though she were instructing children. "Does that make sense?"

<*Tremon, it didn't make any sense at all. Is that on me or her,*> Rika asked privately.

<*I couldn't say. I fell asleep halfway through. I used to think she was shrewd…. I wonder if she just bored people to get her way. I mean, seriously. We don't need to worry about a ten-year plan for defense buildup against Nietzschea.*>

Rika resisted the urge to nod. <*And you'd think we hadn't told her that five or six times.*>

<*I think it was eight.*>

<*Leslie,*> Rika hoped the woman had good news. <*Have you got that trigger device squared away?*>

<*Working on it.*> The captain's tone was clipped. <*More baddies here than we expected, and we're still working out exactly what we have. I think it might be a system that will allow wide-band Link takeover so that everyone will get the transmission. I'm not sure it would work that well, but Jenisa is planting nano on it so Piper can take a look inside.*>

<*I have an initial interface,*> Piper joined in the conversation. <*The system identifies itself as KK100, whatever that is.*>

Rika could feel Tremon stiffen at her side, and she glanced

at him. He was still talking with Arla and Oda as though nothing was wrong, but there was a tightness around his eyes.

<*Are you sure,*> he asked.

<*It's stamped into the console,*> Leslie replied. <*What is it?*>

<*A device…a device that's used to drop mechs where they stand. We built a vulnerability into all of you that could be used to seize control of your bodies and render you unconscious.*>

Rika's lips pressed together, almost disappearing entirely. <*Tremon, we have to talk about secrets later.*>

<*I thought they were all destroyed! We didn't want them to fall into the hands of the Niets when they took Genevia. We still hoped we could hold onto a few systems at that point, and mechs were key to the strategy. In her position, Arla knew everything about the mech program. She must have grabbed one or knew where one was stashed.*>

His apology sounded heartfelt, but she still couldn't help but feel a hint of betrayal that he'd never mentioned anything about the KK100 devices.

When she didn't reply, he added, <*There are…a lot of things I wish I hadn't done. I'll try to think of others I need to bring up. I've just spent a lot of time repressing them.*>

<*No.*> Rika's thoughts briefly touched on several memories she'd rather not have. <*Don't go sifting through your recollections for a litany of sins. We all have them, and dragging them up isn't helpful.*>

<*OK…but I'll try to think of ones pertinent to the mech program. It would be good to get some of it off my chest.*>

Rika and Tremon had shared their last few thoughts privately, and she quickly addressed Leslie and Piper, who she knew would be waiting.

<*Looks like that thing knocks out mechs. A bit of a final solution for us, should we go rogue.*>

<*It won't work,*> Niki said with a laugh. <*What a bunch of idiots.*>

<Are you sure?> Rika asked her AI. *<I assume you think that with our Mark 4 upgrades from the ISF, we're no longer vulnerable to whatever the KK100 does.>*

*<Yeah, they left your bio interfaces the same, so your bodies **feel** the same as they did before, but for all intents and purposes, the ISF rebuilt all the mechs from the ground up.>*

<But they didn't exactly put full-scale ISF tech into us,> Rika countered. *<They had to make sure that we were still field-repairable by our own people.>*

<True…>

Piper sent what he likely thought was a throat-clearing sound, but which came across more like a chair being dragged across the floor. *<We need to treat it like a threat. Maybe it does nothing, maybe it kills you all. I'm working on disabling the device.>*

<And we're still searching for who or what might be the message trigger, if there is such a thing. We might have misinterpreted the intel—Shit! Contacts!>

Leslie sent a 'hold' signal over the Link, and Rika turned her focus back to Arla and Oda, trusting her team to do their jobs without her mothering them.

<Piper, let me know the second you have the KK100 disabled.>

<Think I'd keep it a secret or something?>

Rika suppressed a groan. *<You've been around us too long. Your sarcasm is showing.>*

<Never.> The AI's tone was resolute.

<You never show sarcasm?>

<I could never be around you too long.>

Something in the AI's tone set Rika to wondering if there was a double meaning she didn't quite grasp. Then Oda drew her attention with an especially ridiculous statement.

"It would be best for the Genevian people if you stood down, Rika, and turned over command of your mechs to a proper military authority."

She didn't even bother holding in the laugh that burst past her lips. "Are you serious? Is there something in the water the servitor brought you?"

Oda's ever-present frown deepened. "Yes, I am serious. So far as the GAF is concerned, you are not an officer. You cannot command your forces."

Rika leant forward, knowing the menace her armored and armed body portrayed with such a gesture. "Oda. There *is* no GAF. At present, I represent a mercenary company that is employed by the Scipio Alliance to defeat the Nietzscheans. I'm a Theban citizen—all my mechs were granted citizenship there after we helped save them from the Niets. That means I'm not under your jurisdiction in any way, shape or form."

"But you're Genevian," Oda protested.

"There *is* no Genevia." Tremon's voice was calm and measured. "At least, not yet."

<*Don't tip our hand too soon,*> Rika cautioned.

<*I'm not, I'm distracting him. He's going to try to ferret out what I mean before he does anything drastic.*>

"What do you mean by that?" Oda demanded of Tremon, as predicted.

The former president shrugged. "I just mean that there's no actual nation yet. No one is legally a Genevian citizen. We're also going to need to think of what to do regarding people who were born in Old Genevia during the Nietzschean occupation. Are they Genevian? Does parentage denote citizenship for those people? The letter of the law—the laws we had, at least—was not entirely clear on situations like that."

"We have enough to go on," Oda replied. "And don't forget, The Refuge maintained a government in absentia during the occupation, which is why it makes the most sense to officially declare it to be the interim government."

<*I've been re-examining the intel that landed Leslie at that warehouse,*> Niki said to Rika. <*It was all talking about 'the*

signal', which we interpreted as a trigger for his announcement that he was the new president, yada yada. It always seemed odd that he'd need it—unless he wanted to make sure that his proclamation would get onto all the feeds.>

<Which he could do with a bunch of queued messages on the networks,> Rika responded. *<One doesn't really need a dedicated device for that.>*

<Exactly. And it's not like anyone is going to censor this information. If he makes the announcement, it'll spread like wildfire.>

Rika nodded slowly. *<So you think that he just has to send a 'go' command over the Link, and his message will go out?>*

<I do. I mean…it's what I would do.>

<Me too.>

Tremon was arguing the validity of Oda's 'government in absentia' on the grounds that it had been set up without his knowledge while he was still president—albeit after the elected government had fled the Genevia System. Oda's point was that he'd had no knowledge of the status of the elected government, so his was not established in bad faith.

Rika let them continue to talk as she considered what her next move should be.

<Should we just kill the Link here?> she suggested.

<What if the KK100 has a deadman's switch connected to Oda?> Niki countered. *<We can't make a move on him until Piper disables it.>*

Though her expression was serene—as much so as she could make it—inside, Rika seethed. She had actual work to do, from resupplying her fleet to cementing her position as queen, and all of that was a means to an end. It was the creation of a stable platform from which to launch her attack on Nietzschea. Striking at their heart would cause the empire to pull its assets from Old Genevia without fighting over every system one by one—it would help the Genevian people more than anything, but fools like Oda couldn't see past their own ego far enough to realize that.

Things were growing more heated between Oda and Tremon, while Arla leaned on her sofa's arm with a smirk on her lips.

"Maybe we should take a break," Rika said while rising. "There's no need for us to fight this much. We all want what's best for Genevia."

What she didn't say was that both sides believed that the other was not a part of any viable solution.

"No." Oda spoke the word with calm resolution. "It's clear to me that you won't be useful to the Genevian people any longer. It's time for you to stand down."

<Piper! Where are you on that thing?>

<I'm in, just about to cut power to the transmission array. It's been tricky…there's a lot of interference from all the shooting. Leslie's team almost has things in hand.>

Rika knew she was on the clock. Oda's people had to have alerted him to the fact that there was fighting near the KK100. He wouldn't wait much longer to activate it.

"You're willing to go up against the Scipio Alliance?" she asked. "Don't forget that Admiral Carson is still here. He won't look kindly on this."

Oda shrugged. "We're the legal government of Genevia. By your own admission, you're a mercenary organization employed by a foreign power. You won't submit to our authority, and you won't leave. Legally, I'm within my rights."

He said the word with a note of finality then folded his arms across his chest.

"Umm…your rights to do what?" Rika asked. *<Piper?>*

<It's still online, but I've disabled the transmission array. There's an external connection to the KK100, but so far as whoever is on the other end can tell, the device is fully operational.>

A smug smile settled on Oda's lips. "To do this."

Nothing happened for a moment, and then Piper cried out, <*Oh shit!*>

<*What?*> Rika and Niki demanded at the same time.

<*Kor just got hit by a huge rail slug, tore his legs clean off.*>

<*Dammit, Piper!*> Rika exclaimed before drawing a deep breath and nodding toward Shoshin and Kelly. "These two are under arrest."

"Oda..." Arla breathed the word with an air of menace.

He hung his head. "Shit."

Tremon rose to stand beside Rika. "You probably should have just used your KK100 right from the get-go, not come here to grandstand."

"Don't you see?" Oda's expression lost all of its former poise. "You could have been allies of Genevia, helped us. If only you'd return to your former place."

"I feel the same way," Rika ground out. "But now you'll have a new place. In a prison cell."

"What are the charges?" Arla demanded. "On what grounds are you going to arrest us?"

"Breach of Section 2 of the Phobos Accords," Rika replied. "For starters, at least. However, Marauder regs allow me to hold anyone for as long as necessary in an active combat zone, and because there's no recognized government in Genevia, it still qualifies as active combat by our regs."

"You fu—" Oda began to say as he rose to his feet, but suddenly, Keli appeared before him.

"I'm going to need you to turn and place your hands behind your back."

Oda and Arla both fell silent, and their two guards—who had been eyeing Kelly's GNR during the entire meeting—surrendered without a fight.

<*How're things down there, Leslie,*> Rika asked.

<Oh just peachy keen, thanks for asking. We have medivac coming for Kor, and we're searching through all the intel we found. There was a hidden room that was being used as a CIC, and we found a small store of antimatter.>

<Damn!> Rika exclaimed. *<Really? Think it's the same as what got used in Jague?>*

<The ISF techs confirmed that so long as the antimatter is anti-protium, there's no way to tell whether the stuff in Caleb's bomb was the same as what took out the columns on Pandora Tower. However, they both used the same isotope blend of uranium for their normal matter, so either someone has a firesale of uranium going on—which isn't entirely out of the question—or they're linked.>

Rika's lips twisted as she watched Oda and Arla being led away. *<OK, good work. Get back here when you can. We need to figure out our next move.>*

<You bet, My Queen.>

<Thanks, Pleb.>

Leslie laughed and closed the connection.

<Niki, can—>

<I've already called in Detective Kora. I'm going to sell tickets to watch what she does with those two.>

<You really ***can*** *read my mind, can't you?>*

Niki laughed. *<Maybe a smidge.>*

ULTIMATUM

STELLAR DATE: 06.01.8950 (Adjusted Years)
LOCATION: Mount Genevia, Belgium
REGION: Genevia System, New Genevian Alliance

Rika turned her back on Luxom's orb as it dipped behind the mountains, to face Tremon, Leslie, Chase, Barne, and Silva. She leant against the balcony's railing and drew a deep breath.

"So from the looks of it, Xa was just a red herring. Oda was behind both of the attacks on the parade."

"Or Xa was doing a bit of work on the side to help Oda," Silva suggested. "I mean, seriously. If you were the Niets, who would you want in power—Rika or Oda?"

"I can't even bear to hear those two options presented together," Leslie muttered. "It's also possible that Xa got left behind and did a favor for someone to get a ride out of Genevia."

"Or it was all a smoke screen that Caleb dropped for us," Barne suggested. "Guy's a class-A asswipe."

"Right." Chase set his elbow on the master sergeant's shoulder and leant on the man. "We get how much you dislike him. Point is, someone got this antimatter down here. So who was it?"

Leslie shrugged. "I don't know that we'll ever find out. There's so much contraband flying around right now, it's a miracle no one's blown up a moon by accident."

"Which brings us to our main problem: establishing law and order. Where are we with General Klen?"

<*Do you mean General Mior?*> Niki asked with a soft laugh. <*He's getting his flotilla in order out by Capeton. Once it's all spaceworthy and ready to fly to Belgium, he'll make the proclamation that his is the largest Genevian military in the system, making him*

the magnus, then he'll issue a few orders, plus promote Barne. That'll kick the whole thing off.>

"So close!" Rika's tone was wistful, and a little worried.

"You're not concerned about being in charge, still, are you?" Barne asked. "I thought you were over that."

Rika drew her brows up as she regarded Barne, then laughed. "You know…there's still that thing we did back at Cheri's Villa on Pyra. The thing you don't want shared."

Leslie turned to Barne and folded her arms across her chest. "A thing you two did?"

The master sergeant fixed Rika with a cold stare. "You know, talking *about* it is pretty much the same thing as telling it."

"Oh!" Rika said brightly. "In that case…."

"OK, stop!" Barne shouted. "No need for that to get around."

Leslie glanced at Rika. "It wasn't sex, was it?"

A snort burst from Rika's lips. "Sex? Stars, no. Do you remember how much Barne and I hated each other back then?"

"Uhh…I am right here," Barne said.

"I hate to actually bring you all back on topic," Tremon spoke into the moment of silence that followed, "but does this mean that we're just putting the whole parade assassination thing to rest? Assuming the threat has passed?"

"No," Leslie shook her head vigorously. "Kora's doing her thing with Oda—and it's priceless, she's watching kids' vid feeds with him—and then she's going to pay another visit to Caleb. We'll keep digging there till I'm satisfied that there's nothing left to learn. Then we'll—"

<*Rika,*> Captain Heather's voice came across the command channel. <*A ship just jumped in from the Gerra System. They say that the Nietzscheans are pulling out.*>

<*Seriously?*> Rika asked. <*That's great. Why don't you sound*

excited?>

<Because Captain Becky is saying that they're nuking everything with wild abandon as they go.>

<Shit! ***Everything****?>*

The team on the balcony were all staring at one another with wide eyes.

<She seems a bit…excitable. I'm trying to get more concrete information. It may not be as bad as she's making it out to be.>

"If the Niets are doing this everywhere…" Chase spoke the words softly, though the thought was already on everyone's mind.

"They wouldn't," Barne shook his head. "Some systems they'd hold onto for strategic reasons, make us fight for them. The Niets don't run, so this is a different sort of strategy."

"OK," Rika nodded. "You're right, the Niets don't fight like that. If they're blasting systems as they go, it wouldn't be wholesale destruction, they'd want to make it hurt more for us."

<They're creating humanitarian crises to slow you down, buy time for them to build up a stronger defense,> Niki said. *<And it'll work, too. We're going to have to send aid to all the nearby systems.>*

"All?" Rika asked.

"If they did this at Gerra, they probably did it at others," Chase said. "Sending aid or taking in refugees from just one system is manageable. Three, five, ten? That starts to become the work of years."

"Fuckers," Rika muttered.

Leslie nodded. "They *are* Nietzscheans. They fight dirty. It's how they won the war the first time."

"Well, not this time," Rika said. *<Piper, relay to Vargo that I want him to kick off his roadshow now. Tell him to make his proclamations, and start his promotions. We need to send aid, and counterattack immediately.>*

She had sent the message over the command channel, and the team standing around her appeared puzzled.

"Counterattack where?" Barne asked.

A holo appeared in front of the group, centered on Genevia and the systems around it.

"OK…I know we won't be ready immediately, but I want them to think that's our plan. Let's just say that the Niets do their little scorched earth routine on these five systems." As she spoke, five of the star systems closest to Genevia lit up. "They have at least two thousand ships, maybe more, spread across these five systems. If they get word that we're sending resources, military and otherwise, for aid, what do you think they'll do?"

"They're gonna swoop and poop," Barne muttered.

"They'll what?" Tremon asked, a look of mild disgust on his face.

Rika laughed at the term, but understood the master sergeant's meaning.

"They can't take and hold the Genevia System with those ships," she explained. "Especially not while we have the ISF on hand. However, they can certainly fly through the outer system here and wreak some serious havoc. Then we start off our New Genevia with six star systems that are crippled and all but defenseless."

"Which is exactly why you didn't want to spread out in the first place," Chase said. "This keeps us from striking out at Nietzschea."

Rika nodded while calling up to Heather, *<Anything else?>*

<They're still several light hours out, so it'll take a bit for more information. They did send a short data feed of nukes hitting Gepa and a few stations. It's bad, but I don't think the Niets are going for total destruction.>

"So just what we feared, then." Silva shook her head in dismay. "What are we going to do?"

Rika ran a hand through her hair. "We have to stick to the plan. We're going to need to render what aid we can, but bolster this system's outer defenses while we prepare to hit Nietzschea."

<Rika.>

The message came from Admiral Carson, and the tone in his mental voice set her teeth on edge.

<Admiral Carson, what is it?>

<New Canaan is under attack. My fleet has been called home. The ships at the jump gates are already on their way out of Genevia. I'm ten hours from jump at max boost, so whatever you need me to do, it has to happen by then.>

Rika felt her stomach drop. She was certain that they could square away everything with the transfer of Marauder assets by then, but with the Niets running a scorched earth campaign, she'd been counting on the ISF fleet to back her up.

<Shit, Niki, what are we going to do?>

<New Canaan is the ISF's home system. They're going to defend it with everything they have. Carson will be back before long.>

That eventuality felt less certain to Rika.

<I understand, Admiral. We've already started our shenanigans here. We'll let you know when General Barne is in command of the Marauders. Who…who are the attackers?>

She asked the question, but almost didn't want to know. Any enemy who felt brave enough to launch an assault on New Canaan was one she didn't want to go up against.

Carson's reply took a few seconds longer than Rika had hoped.

<We don't know. Let me know when I need to approve the orders.>

<Understood, will do.>

Rika's focus shifted back to the people standing before her. They were all staring at her silently, and she swallowed before speaking.

"Carson just reached out. New Canaan is under attack, and he's been called back."

"Shit!" Barne muttered. "What does that mean?"

A part of Rika wanted to run and hide, to take her Marauders and find some quiet corner of the galaxy. The strength of the ISF was a cornerstone of her belief that they could actually take on the Nietzscheans….

But as she felt that fear set in, she remembered the vision Tangel had given her, of the rock that sheltered others in the midst of a raging storm.

I am that rock.

"We do what we have to do," she said in a low voice. "We've beaten back the Niets before, without the ISF's help. We bested them at Hercules, Sepe, Blue Ridge, and Iberia." With each system name she listed, her team nodded, their backs straightening. "If they think that their cowardly tactics are going to weaken our resolve, they're sorely mistaken. We're Marauders, and they fear us."

"Well…in a few hours, we're all going to be NGSF," Chase corrected with a wink.

"Way to take the wind out of our sails," Silva muttered.

"You know…" Tremon spoke up, tapping a finger against his chin. "I didn't know General Mill personally, but I remember the reports of how hard he fought at the end of the war—I felt like a part of Genevia was alive in his mercenary company. He founded the Marauders out of the remains of the Genevian military. Maybe it should just *be* the Genevian military."

"Would that cause any legal issues?" Leslie asked.

"Maybe we could officially be the Genevian Marauders," Chase suggested. "I really don't feel like I'm ready to give that up to be the New Genevian Space Force."

Something clicked in place inside Rika, and she nodded.

"Yes. That feels right. Being Marauders is in our blood now, there's no leaving it behind."

"To the Genevian Marauders!" Barne thrust a fist in the air, and the others followed suit, shouting the name.

When the excitement died down, Rika looked over the men and women before her, their eyes growing sober once more. They reached a wordless understanding: the road ahead would be long and hard, but they would have each other, and the Genevian Marauder family to sustain them.

"OK, people," Rika said in a voice still choked with emotion. "We have work to do."

THE QUEEN

STELLAR DATE: 06.02.8950 (Adjusted Years)
LOCATION: Mount Genevia, Belgium
REGION: Genevia System, New Genevian Alliance

Twelve hours later, shortly after dawn, Rika stood in the audience room in the Royal Estate atop Mount Genevia.

Admiral Carson and the ISF forces had left the system, gone to fight the mysterious enemy that had beset New Canaan. Rumors were flying as to who it could be, but Rika knew the list of possible foes to be short.

Though I suppose it could be all of them at once.

Even so, those gathered atop the mountain were putting on a good face, determined to mark the occasion with high spirits. A host of civilians was present, many of which Rika knew to some degree from interactions over the past few weeks, but they were the backdrop. It was her Marauders, the mechs and humans of her battalion whose gazes she met, one after the other, as they beamed at her with pride writ large on their features.

Ironically, that moment, none of them were Marauders…not exactly.

Vargo Klen, in his new-old persona of General Mior, had given Barne a special field promotion to General, and Rika had resigned her commission—something that had been far more emotional than she'd expected.

Vargo had then reinstated Rika in the newly formed NGSF and promoted her clear up to a three-star general.

She was certain that someone writing the history books would laugh at the shenanigans they'd pulled to get to this point, but the most important thing was that—thanks to a mountain of documentation—everything they were doing was entirely legal under Old Genevian law.

So now she stood, a general in the NGSF, before the Genevian magnus, who had ruled for all of twelve hours, in front of the people she had fought and bled alongside for the past two years of her life.

"Are you ready?" Vargo asked in a voice barely above a whisper. "I could still commission Oda and make him magnus."

Rika snorted and shook her head. "You don't need to goad me into a coup, *General Mior*. I'm finally ready for this. Just…just get on with it before I lose my nerve."

Vargo nodded. "General Rika of the New Genevian Space Force, I have a matter of grave importance to discuss with you."

Hearing the reference to the NGSF grated on Rika's ears, but by the time they'd settled on Genevian Marauders, Vargo had already disseminated the other name. It made no matter, though. She'd rename the military as one of her first acts.

"General Mior, I stand ready for whatever task you have for me."

They'd not rehearsed the words, but Rika decided to have a little fun with it. Something to mark the memory.

"It won't be easy," he replied, his voice ringing out and filling the room. "But it's a job fit for a queen."

She rolled her eyes at him, but replied in a somber voice. "I'm not afraid of a difficult assignment."

"Good." He reached into a pouch on his waist and pulled out a sheet of plas. "This is my resignation from the NGSF, effective immediately. I am no longer the head of the Genevian military, and I am no longer the Genevian magnus. You are, General Rika."

Rika took the plas, nodding silently as a feeling of nervous uncertainty welled up inside of her. Applause came from around the room, and she felt a lump form in her throat. She turned from Vargo to face those assembled, and a smile split her lips, growing so wide it ached.

<*Stars, woman,*> Niki laughed in her mind. <*You were born for this.*>

<*What about you?*> Rika asked.

<*Me? I'm just along for the ride. Take some pictures, add a bit to my diary, make sure your head doesn't get blown off.*>

Rika laughed and shook her head, raising her hands for silence—which only made the cheering grow louder. She saw that even the normally stoic Tremon was shouting and clapping his hands above his head.

It took several minutes for the furor to die down, and when it did, Rika called out, "Now where's that Vargo Klen?"

"Here, Magnus Rika," he said from beside her.

"Ah, yes. Well, I'm sorry to say, but you've just been drafted. But since I heard that you quit the Marauders all willy-nilly, I'm going to have to reinstate you as a captain."

The man beamed at her and nodded while shaking her hand. "That'll do just fine, ma'am."

"And as for the rest of you," Rika shouted above the din that ensued. "We're not calling this outfit the NGSF—sorry, Captain Heather. You're all in the Genevian Marauders now!"

This time it took a shorter period for the cheers to die down, but more because everyone was hoarse than from a lack of excitement.

"Now, you're all thirsty after screaming," Rika continued, "so as my second act, I'm telling you all to enjoy yourselves—but not too much. We have a football game this afternoon."

She felt a modicum of guilt that they'd have the game without Colonel Borden's ISF Marines, but they'd returned to New Canaan with Admiral Carson, none of them able to sit by idly as their home system was under attack.

The only silver lining was that they'd left their massive

walker, the Starcrusher, behind.

The ranks of soldiers and crowd of civilians broke up at her words and began to mill about, talking and enjoying beverages the servitors began to pass around. Even though everyone appeared pleased with the proceedings, there was a pall hanging over the attendees. Ships from two more systems had jumped in during the night, telling of other systems that had seen the Nietzscheans cripple their infrastructure and destroy food supplies before they left.

She was tempted not to have the football game, but Tremon had convinced her that it was worth it, and the reports from intel indicated that they'd still have time to move the fleets to defensive positions before the Nietzscheans could launch an attack on Genevia—should they plan to.

"Well, Magnus," Chase said as he approached Rika. "You've finally done it."

"This was just a ceremony," she replied, taking his hands in hers. "There's still so much to do."

"I think that'll always be the case, but this calls for a bit of contentment, don't you think? Just for a moment?"

Rika nodded, smiling at the man standing before her. "Yeah, I suppose…though I'm going to hold out hope that at *some* point, things settle down a bit."

"You wouldn't know what to do if they did," he replied.

Rika nodded as she looked out over those assembled around them. "You're probably right. But can I pretend for a bit?"

"Sure, we all have our little fantasies."

<*Magnus,*> Piper spoke into Rika's mind before she could reply to Chase.

<*You don't always have to call me that.*>

<*OK, but the* Pinnacle *is moving, and I can't raise it.*>

<*What?*>

Piper fed her the scan data, which showed the *Pinnacle,* the massive carrier that the Nietszcheans had been building at the Capeton shipyards, boosting away from the planet on an outsystem vector.

<*I didn't order that,*> Rika said, trying to absorb what she was seeing.

<*I know that,*> the AI replied. <*I also think I have an idea why the Niets were building that thing.*>

THE LANCE

STELLAR DATE: 06.02.8950 (Adjusted Years)
LOCATION: GMS *Fury Lance,* departing Belgium
REGION: Genevia System, New Genevian Alliance

Rika leant over the holotank on the bridge of the *Fury Lance* and shook her head in disbelief.

"How the hell did the Niets get tech like this?" she asked.

<*I can only assume that it was from Orion,*> Niki suggested. <*General Garza must have provided them the plans.*>

"I guess that explains why it's so weird," Captain Heather said.

"Yeah." Rika ran a hand through her hair as she stared at the six-kilometer-long ship with its single central hull surrounded by six cantilevered hulls. She'd always assumed that the vessel was designed that way just to fit through smaller jump gates and present a smaller mass profile for regular FTL flight.

However, the central hull had a two-hundred-meter void that hadn't served any discernable purpose until Piper correlated information that Kora had gotten from Oda and Arla with what he knew of black holes.

<*I could still be wrong,*> Piper said. <*It could be something else, but if I am wrong….*>

"I think everything else has been a smoke screen," Rika said. "When properly outfitted, that ship has the ability to smash stasis shields, and if those ancillary hulls do what you think, it can steer the beam it fires."

Heather met her gaze. "Which means that if the Niets manage to escape with it, and can replicate the tech, our biggest tactical advantage disappears."

"Or we're forced to attack prematurely to stop them from

building more," Rika replied. "Either way, it sucks."

Silva stood a meter away, studying the secondary holotank, which displayed the positions of the Marauder fleets in the Genevia System. "A lotta sucks. We were stretched thin even when Carson was here. Most of our ships have skeleton crews at best. I hope to hell that the Niets aren't good enough at timing things to pull off their swoop and poop in the next day or so. We're gonna get caught with our pants around our ankles."

"You don't wear pants," Heather countered. "One of the benefits of being a mech."

Silva gave a single laugh and rolled her eyes. "You're a funny one. Still, I suppose we don't even know for certain that it's the Niets who're making off with the *Pinnacle*. There were only a dozen engineers and a pair of LHO mechs on board. It wouldn't have taken a large force to take the ship."

"And then be able to pilot it?" Rika asked. "It's one thing to board a ship like that. It's something else entirely to have it be anything other than a big hunk of steel in space."

"Sure," Heather nodded in agreement. "But keep in mind those engineers know how to fly the ship, and civilians aren't trained to resist torture."

"The *Pinnacle* is worth more than a planet," Silva said. "I can guarantee you that if the opportunity presented itself, there are a lot of enterprising individuals who would have gleefully stolen the thing."

"Valid," Rika said. "Either way, we have to assume that it has a competent crew."

"Which is why I wish we weren't chasing after it alone," Silva said. "I get that we have to anchor all our other defensive positions with stasis-shielded ships, but I'd feel a hell of a lot better if it wasn't just us versus that behemoth."

Heather cleared her throat and patted the side of the holotank. "Don't you besmirch my *Lance*, Colonel Silva. I won't have it."

"I'm not besmirching," Silva protested. "It's just that that thing is four times our mass and has a main weapon that can fire right through our stasis shields."

<*It's not active.*> Piper's voice was calm and unconcerned. <*We don't have to worry about it breaching our stasis shields.*>

"How sure are you about that?" Silva asked.

<*Utterly. Black holes have a lot of mass…as you well know. If there was one inside the* Pinnacle*—even a small one—we'd be able to tell by the ship's thrust alone.*>

"Did the ISF provide any data on how big the black hole has to be to power the anti-stasis beam?" Rika asked.

Though the Nietzscheans had never before fielded a ship with weapons capable of breaching stasis shields, the ISF had encountered them several times. They called them DMG ships, and the first had been produced by a now-defunct faction in the war called Airtha. Later, the Orion Guard had demonstrated that they also possessed DMG weaponry.

Because the beams a DMG ship could fire were capable of holing even one of the ISF's vaunted I-Class super-dreadnoughts, DMG technology was something about which they didn't disclose a lot of details.

Niki confirmed that expectation. <*No, they never gave out any information about what size the black hole has to be. But even one the size of your fist weighs as much as a planet, so they do tend to be noticeable.*>

"And what if it only has to be microscopic?" Rika asked.

The three women shared a long look while they waited for one of the AIs to respond.

<*Well, we'd still see it in their thrust profile,*> Piper said. <*The ship masses exactly what it should. Even a black hole a micrometer across weighs as much as the* Pinnacle. *We'd certainly notice that.*>

Rika knew that, but it was nice to hear Piper confirm it, and put the fear that she'd missed some critical part of the equation to rest.

"I guess that makes me feel better."

"So," Silva gestured to her holotank, which showed the *Pinnacle*'s outsystem route and the *Fury Lance*'s intercept route. "At our current acceleration, we'll meet them just as they pass Babylon. They're obviously going to use it for a gravity assist, so if we don't take them then, they'll make it to jump distance."

"No pressure," Heather muttered.

Rika laughed. "Just another day at the office."

"You've never worked at an office, Rika," Silva shot back, her tone terse.

For a moment, Rika was about to respond in kind, but she bit her tongue. Silva's daughter, Amy, was aboard Tangel's flagship, the *I2*. There was no doubt in anyone's mind that if New Canaan was under attack, that's where the *I2* would be.

"Good point," Rika said after a moment of mental floundering.

"We'll hit them here." Heather placed a marker on the holotank's display, just past where the other ship would emerge from its slingshot maneuver. "We'll fire everything we have at their engines. Even at full power, their shields won't be able to take the *Lance*'s atom beams—not unless they turn the ship at the last moment to move their engines away from us."

"And that ship turns slow, so even the *Lance* can outmaneuver it," Rika added. "Then we storm it."

"OK, then," Heather said. "We just have twenty-two hours until intercept. Anyone have a Snark deck handy?"

A GAME OF SNARK

STELLAR DATE: 06.03.8950 (Adjusted Years)
LOCATION: GMS *Fury Lance*, en route to Babylon
REGION: Genevia System, New Genevian Alliance

"Shit!" Leslie swore, shaking her head in disgust. "You've been captain for six voyages so far, Rika. How do you do that?"

"I don't know," Chase added, giving Rika a suspicious glare. "But if she had sleeves, I'd suspect something was up them."

"It's just six voyages," she replied, picking up the cards from the best manifest and setting them in the cargo pile before shuffling the rest back together. "One time, Barne held it for over thirty."

"By cheating," Leslie growled.

"Shouldn't you be supporting your partner?" Rika teased.

"I do. Trust me, being with Barne requires a lot of supporting. But he was totally cheating that time. I don't know how, but he even admitted it to me."

"No way." Chase shook his head. "I was watching him like a hawk, he couldn't have been."

Leslie shrugged. "Well, he claims he was, and while I often wouldn't, this time I believe him."

"He does like to mess with people," Rika said. "It would be *so* Barne to tell people he was cheating when he wasn't, just to make them go nuts trying to figure out what he'd done that he didn't actually do."

"Yeah, that would fit as well." The other woman nodded in agreement.

"What do you see in him, anyway?" Chase asked as he picked up the cards Rika dealt.

Leslie's tail swished in the air behind her, and she gave Chase a languid wink. "Maybe I'm with him just to get you to ask me why I'm with him. Ever think of that?"

"No, because I didn't think you were that much of a masochist."

Leslie snorted. "You're hilarious."

"Are you ever going to stop asking Leslie why she's with Barne?" Rika picked up her cards and looked over them at Chase. "You're going to give me a complex."

"It does come off a bit like you want to bang me," Leslie said as she pulled out her two best cards and passed them to Rika.

"Whoa, hey," Chase gave Leslie a wide-eyed look before shaking his head. "That's not what I was going for at all. It's like a mystery of the universe, you know. Like why some stars don't have Oort clouds, or whether or not low-mass primordial black holes can survive from one universe to the next."

"As much as I like being compared to a black hole, I—"

"Well, you've modded your skin to be very dark," Chase interrupted. "I mean…so much innuendo is possible right now."

Leslie locked eyes with Rika. "Is he trying Barne-level humor now?"

"Beats me. Here are your two cards. I hope you like them."

"You're all grace, Your Grace."

"I don't think queens get called 'Your Grace'," Rika said. "Well, maybe?"

"Pretty sure it's priests that get called that," Chase said as he sorted through the cards in his hand.

Rika played a pair of sixes, and he pulled out two cards and was about to set them down on the table, when his eyes flicked up and turned to the galley's entrance.

"About time, Bondo. I was dragging this game out as long

as I could."

"Sorry, Captain," the lieutenant said from behind Rika, and she turned to see the head of the company's Repair and Refit team grinning like a fool.

"Dragged it out, why?" she asked suspiciously.

"Well, you see..." Bondo began slowly, suddenly looking uncertain of himself.

"It's your armor," Chase said, placing his cards on the table and rising to stand beside the R&R lieutenant. "There was something wrong with it."

Rika's brows knit together. "Something wrong with it? But you repaired it after that fight on Lisbon. It seemed fine when I wore it after."

"Well, of *course*." Bondo's expression shifted from one of uncertainty to pure confidence. "I wouldn't screw up repairs on *your* armor."

"So then, what's wrong with it?" Rika pressed.

"Well..." Chase said, glancing at the lieutenant. "Is it the color, specifically?"

"A bit, yeah."

"Wait," Rika held up a hand as she glanced down at herself. "It's stealth armor, it can *change* color."

"The design, then," Bondo said with a nod. "Yeah, color and design. They go hand-in-hand, you know."

"OK, you two, what's going on?" she demanded, a smile on her lips. "You're clearly up to something."

"Bring it in," the lieutenant called over his shoulder.

A second later, Corporal Stripes came into view, pushing an armor rack on an a-grav pad into the galley. The rack held what was clearly SMI gear, but it wasn't the standard grey, it was white—though not a pure white, more of an eggshell.

But that wasn't the only difference. Instead of being blocky and angular, it was slimmer. More human-looking. A GNR sat on the rack, its design matching the armor: sleeker, with the ammo mounts further back, atop rather than below the firing system.

"Something fit for a queen, perhaps," Bondo said nervously.

Rika glanced at Chase, whose lips pulled back in a broad smile, and then at Leslie, who looked as surprised as she did.

"Do you like it?" Chase prompted.

<*You have to say something,*> Niki whispered into Rika's mind.

<*Did you know about this?*>

<*Of course I did. And I know you like it, so tell them.*>

Rika nodded and swallowed before speaking. "Yeah…it's amazing. Um…just one question. It still stealths, right?"

Bondo barked a laugh. "Of course, General. We want you to look like a queen, not get your head blown off in our next engagement."

<*Which is going to be sooner than we thought.*> Piper's voice came over the general shipnet. <*Our prey isn't using Babylon for a gravity assist. They've turned and are braking.*>

"Going to ground, then," Rika said, her eyes still on the armor. "I guess I might just get to try this out today."

"You thinking about a breach, like when we took the *Lance*?" Leslie asked.

"Got it in one," Rika replied. "Time to kick the door in."

BABYLON

STELLAR DATE: 06.03.8950 (Adjusted Years)
LOCATION: GMS *Fury Lance,* Babylon
REGION: Genevia System, New Genevian Alliance

"You sure about this?" Chase asked as he inspected Rika's armor. "You're the magnus now, all special and important."

"This is what I do," she replied, looking down at the white plates that covered her body. Even though she had grown quite accustomed to the matte grey of the ISF flow armor, she was already enamored with her new look. "I lead from the front."

He nodded, both in agreement and in pronouncement that he was satisfied with her gear. "You know that history suggests it's not an ideal long-term strategy."

Rika shrugged. "I've always been on the front. It's where I see things best. And besides, Piper and Heather will be here on the *Lance*. They're our eyes in the sky."

"It's *all* sky out there," Chase replied. "And storms, and lightning, and dragons and shit."

"Just a gas giant. Been there, done that."

"You've never dived into a gas giant with dragons."

Rika fixed Chase with a serious stare. "Those stories about Babylon are just old spacer nonsense. The only dragons out there are Adira's, and she's still at Parsons. Besides, don't you have a platoon to see to?"

"Chris and Kristian can manage their platoon just fine. Everyone knows I'm along to keep the magnus safe."

"I thought that's what Kelly's fireteam was for."

Chase shrugged. "I guess they finally have their fourth."

"That mean you're finally signing up for the Queen's Guard?"

"Finally?!" Chase laughed. "Rika, I'm the founding member."

"Well, if you want to go all the way back, Silva and Kelly predate you."

"Sure, but to them, you were just another SMI. You were always my queen."

Rika groaned, but leant forward to kiss him anyway. "Why are you so cheesy?" she asked when their lips parted.

"Probably because you're like a fine wine. You need to be paired with a sharp cheese."

"Oh stars…"

"Admit it, you love me, Rika."

"Damn straight I love you." She placed her hand on his shoulders, nudging him to turn so she could inspect his armor. "And just a bit more than kicking Nietzschean ass, too."

"Lucky me."

"Well, I love my gun arm more than either of those things, don't forget that."

Chase snorted and patted the chaingun mounted to his left forearm. "I feel the same about Miss Chitty Bang Bang, but she still lets you come to bed with us."

"Miss Chitty Bang Bang?" Rika asked with a laugh. "Your gun's a girl?"

Chase turned and met her eyes. "The deadliest person I know is a woman. It seemed fitting."

"Aww, you're so sweet."

"I was talking about Tangel."

Rika gave him a playful shove. "I hope you get a leg shot off."

"Then you'll have to carry me."

"I'll hook a tow cable on your armor and drag you. How's that?"

Chase chuckled as he walked to the door and palmed it open. "You drag me everywhere already. Why not move beyond the metaphorical?"

"You like it," Rika countered as she walked out after him.

"In your words—strange as they are—damn straight I do. Now let's go do your second favorite thing."

She shot him a confused look. "You want to do my gun-arm?"

"That was first."

"Oh, well, I guess that means I just promoted you."

Chase reached out and clasped her hand. "Think Miss Chitty Bang Bang can still get it on with your gun arm?"

Rika snorted, then let out a long laugh. "We'll see."

* * * * *

Rika rode a dropship piloted by Chase with Kelly's team in the back. They were on their way to secure one of the aft port bays near engineering. It wasn't a primary target, but would be useful for egress if things went sour on the ship.

The primary assault was being led by Lieutenant Chris, who was taking Squads Two and Three to the bridge. Squad One was being led by Leslie, their target being the main engineering bay.

Leslie had insisted that they lead a team there, as it was where she expected Jeremy and Annie to be—two engineers she'd worked with when they took the *Pinnacle* from the Niets a few weeks ago.

"The *Lance*'s probes have a fix on the ship," Chase called back. "I'm bringing us into the clouds now."

"Got it," Rika called up, flipping the forward displays in the ship to show the wispy, high altitude clouds that shrouded the planet. The shuttle barely twitched as it eased into Babylon's upper atmosphere and past the world's outer sentinels.

Below lay towering cumulous peaks, between which stretched dark, seething valleys that plunged hundreds of kilometers into the planet's atmosphere. Lightning spiderwebbed along the billowing slopes, casting the opposing walls of cloud into stark relief for brief moments before the depths fell into shadow once more.

A marker appeared on the display, noting the location and vector of the *Pinnacle*.

"It's just holding," Kelly muttered. "Why did they race out here to hide in the clouds? They must know that we wouldn't be afraid to come after them."

"Maybe they thought we'd bring the whole fleet," Rika suggested. "Or more of it…expose the rest of the system to attack."

"They don't have quantum communication, though," Shoshin said. "They can't coordinate an attack that well."

"Maybe they're hoping for lady luck to pay them a visit," Keli suggested.

"Doesn't matter." Rika continued to stare at the display as though she could force it to tell her what she wanted to know. "Our mission priorities are unchanged. We take the *Pinnacle* back, or we scuttle it. The Niets won't get this prize."

"Probes lost it," Chase called back. "It moved into a high-pressure zone, shoved them away."

"Can't imagine what it's like to fly that thing down there," Kelly said as the dropship continued to fall toward the next layer of clouds.

"We're going to find out before long," Chase said from the cockpit. "Ah, they spotted it again, shifting vector."

The dropship banked hard to port, and Rika tapped the ship's external sensors to see that the other five craft in their formation had done the same. Though it would be harrowing, their goal was to meet and board the *Pinnacle* inside the clouds. If the ship saw them on close approach, its point defense weapons would spell a quick end to the assault craft.

The next few minutes were spent staring at the displays as tensions rose the further the ships fell. The marker noting the *Pinnacle*'s location showed it to be within a hundred-kilometer-wide tower of ice and ammonia. Based on the last reading the probes had, it would still be well within the cloud when the dropships reached it.

Rika looked to her team, noting how the three mechs straightened under her gaze. "OK, people, here's how—"

"Look!" Chase interrupted, and the four mechs in the back of the dropship turned to the forward displays, more than one gasp being breathed as the bow of the *Pinnacle* surged out of the wall of gas only a hundred kilometers away. Without warning, a beam of white light burst from the vessel's nose, blasting past the dropships and out into space.

Bolts of lightning arched out around the massive ship, and Chase swore as he dove the ship below the twisting streams of energy.

<*Idiots!*> Niki followed the proclamation with a string of curses. <*They can't fire that thing in atmosphere!*>

"Thing?" Kelly whispered. "Did they just fire the DMG?"

<*No other weapon like that on the ship. It has to be.*>

Rika tracked the DMG's angle, and saw one possible target.

"Fuck."

"I can't raise the *Lance*," Chase called back, his voice edged with panic.

"Stay on course," Rika ordered. "We're boarding that ship no matter what."

<*Rika!*> Heather's voice burst into her mind. <*Trying to stabilize our orbit, but they holed us amidships, through and through.*>

<*Don't worry about the* Lance,> she shot back. <*Abandon ship!*>

<I gotta try, Rika.>

<That's an order, Heather. Abandon ship!>

The single word that came back was filled with sorrow.

<Aye.>

"Get us on that thing yesterday," Rika ground out between clenched teeth. "I'm going to pound those assholes into hamburger."

"Fuckin' A," Kelly chimed in.

Chase didn't respond, but the dropship didn't slow as it approached the *Pinnacle,* and she knew he was seething with as much rage as the rest of them. One moment, the ship was kilometers away, and a few seconds later, they'd punched through its grav shields and were between the cantilevered hulls that rotated around the ship's central axis.

The dropship spun, and they were slammed forward into their harnesses as the craft braked, rapidly decelerating to match velocity with the DMG ship. Something slammed into the dropship, and Rika barely had time to wonder if it was a weapon or if something had pulled free from the massive ship as it was buffeted by Babylon's winds, when suddenly, the external views went dark, and the dropship's motion ground to a halt.

"We made it!" Chase called back. "We're in a bay."

"The right bay?" Rika asked, suddenly realizing that a massive hole was torn through the side of the craft. She could make out a dimly lit bay through the rent, heat signatures shifting as atmosphere tore through the hole Chase had punched in the bay's doors on his way in.

"Safe to say they know we're here," Kelly muttered.

<It fired,> Niki whispered.

"Yeah," Rika replied, pulling off her harness and rising from her seat.

<No, you don't follow. It fired ***again.****>*

"Shit," Chase muttered. "Yeah, there it is, in the logs. A

second burst."

<*Heather?*> Rika called out. <Fury Lance, *do you read?*>

<*Could be interference,*> Niki said, though her tone indicated that she didn't believe that to be the case.

Rika wanted to scream, but she sucked in a quivering breath, blew it out, and then repeated the process.

"OK, people. We still have a mission, it's just even more important now. We take the *Pinnacle*. No matter what."

Chase walked out of the cockpit and grabbed his rifle, locking eyes with her. "No matter what."

THE PINNACLE

STELLAR DATE: 06.03.8950 (Adjusted Years)
LOCATION: GMS *Pinnacle*, Babylon
REGION: Genevia System, New Genevian Alliance

Rika checked her corner and signaled Kelly and Keli to move forward, leapfrogging her on their way to engineering, where they were meeting up with Leslie's team.

By some miracle—though one that felt shallow, with the loss of the *Lance*—all of the dropships had breached the *Pinnacle* with all hands, though none at their intended ingress points.

With her team closest to engineering, that became Rika's primary target, Leslie's squad was still headed there, though a few minutes behind.

Their progress was slow, but unimpeded. Niki had breached the ship's surveillance systems, and from what they could see, the vessel was nearly empty. Both the bridge and engineering were displayed as offline on the internal monitors and sensors…something that surprised no one.

Though they were able to move without opposition through the ship, the corridors they'd passed through thus far were unpressurized, which limited the teams' options for drones. Whoever had made the choice to vent atmosphere was familiar with shipboard combat. Drones in atmosphere or zero-*g* were one thing, but when the ship was unpressurized but still had gravity, things became a bit more difficult.

Granted, Rika thought as she moved up on Kelly and Keli, Shoshin and Chase trailing behind, *the ship's a-grav is offline as well. This is Babylon's pull we're feeling.*

Something made obvious by the fact that they were walking on the bulkheads through this stretch of the journey.

<Just thirty meters down this passageway, and then ten down the next, and we're at the starboard doors,> she informed the team.

<We have HUDs too,> Kelly muttered.

<Just making sure we're all on the same page.>

<Sealed bulkhead ahead,> Chase said, highlighting a closed door at the next corner.

<Makes sense,> Rika replied. *<Easier to see us coming if we have to go through an airlock into a pressurized area.>*

<We could just shoot out the doors,> Shoshin suggested. *<Squishies might not be in EV suits.>*

<And if our civilians are in there?> Rika asked.

The AM-4 didn't reply, and his silence told everyone what they'd need to do: what they always did, put their lives on the line to protect people without flowmetal skin.

Rika didn't resent less evolved humans their weaknesses, but she was starting to wish they were better prepared for the dangers the universe threw at them all.

The mechs formed up at the closed door, Chase palming the panel once they were set up. It slid open without protest, and Kelly and Keli moved in. They advanced to the far end, where a closed double door was all that separated them from engineering.

<It's warm,> Kelly reported. *<Atmo in there.>*

<Got it.> Rika signaled the rest of the team to move into the corridor.

Once inside, Chase sealed the door behind them, and she forced down the feeling that they were all standing in a killbox—as much as she could. They were, after all, standing in a killbox.

<I got into the lighting in there,> Niki said. *<I can kill it right before the doors open.>*

<Excellent.>

Rika sidled up behind Kelly, back against the bulkhead as

the SMI-4 waited for the word to open the door. She looked around the passage, not seeing a single mech with her vision, though she knew they were all present.

<OK, everyone. By the numbers, nice and smooth. No headshots—we want people to question. Look out for our engineer friends, we owe them a lot.>

Affirmative responses came back from the other mechs, and Rika sent the signal for Kelly to breach the door.

Half a second before the portal slid open, the lights died, and the team fell back to their IR and backscatter radiation overlays. Then the door was open, air blasting past them as Kelly and Keli moved through the venturi and split up. The other mechs followed a moment later, Rika third-last, only Chase and Shoshin trailing after.

They all maintained EM silence, other than the random IFF pings their armor sent out for positioning. The bay, a large space by any ship's standards, was filled with random noises that Rika's armor filtered out one by one, until all she could hear were small sounds that were too random to safely ignore.

<It can't be a red herring,> she said to Niki. *<There's no way they'd leave engineering unprotected.>*

<Go to the command station in the center,> the AI directed. *<We'll drop a breach kit on that sucker and take helm control. That'll draw them out.>*

Rika nodded, a wry smile on her lips. *<Sounds like a plan.>*

She sent a short burst to the rest of the team, informing them of her destination, and began to move amongst the consoles and stations, carefully tracing a path to the command station. Once there, she crouched near the edge of the elevated platform and placed her hand on the side of a workstation.

A passel of nano flowed out of her hand, and she moved back, waiting for Niki to run her breach.

<OK, I've found an access port. Nano's building an interface.>

Rika nodded, and before she could respond, the lights

snapped back on. Her eyes were drawn to an object on the far side of the command station that she hadn't fully made out in the darkness.

It was a KK100.

A second later, a man appeared in front of it, and the data she had on Nietzschean operatives identified him as Xa.

A toothy smile stretched across his face as he waved at her.

Then everything went dark.

* * * * *

<*Crunch,*> Leslie called out. <*What are you waiting for? Open the doors.*>

There was no response from the squad leader, and Leslie tried to get a response from Corporal Ben, followed by Whispers, Kim, and Harris.

None of the mechs responded. Their armor was still sending out IFF signal, so she knew they hadn't moved. She crept up to where she knew Crunch stood and placed a hand on his shoulder. The armor was perfectly matched to room temperature, but she could feel the slight shift as the mech continued to draw breath.

<*Rika,*> she called out, getting no response from their leader. She tried Lieutenant Chris and the other platoon leaders, getting—as she expected at this point—no response.

KK100.

The word echoed in her mind, and she knew what had happened. Somewhere in the ship, one of those disgusting devices had been used. It seemed, however, that it had just rendered the mechs immobile, not allowed the operator to take control of their bodies.

Small mercies, she thought.

Knowing there was nothing for it, she approached the

door's control panel and activated it. Before it slid aside, she ducked behind Crunch and shoved hard the moment the portal opened.

He toppled over and hit the deck with a thud that echoed through the space beyond.

"Check it out," a voice called out from somewhere within the large bay.

That's right. She eased past Crunch's immobile and invisible form, creeping toward a row of workstations. *Split up, make it nice and easy.*

She spotted a figure standing atop the command center's raised platform, and recognized him as Xa. A string of curses filtered through her mind, some directed at the spy, some at herself for not finding any leads that had led her to him before now.

Leslie let her anger run for a moment, but then tamped it down, releasing a nanocloud into the room and tagging enemies.

She spotted four moving toward where she'd entered the bay, and two more at the far side. Another three were standing with Xa on the platform. They were wearing matte black armor without markings, but she recognized their rifles as Nietzschean spec-ops gear.

It was possible that more were in stealth around the room. Her nanocloud *should* be able to pick them out, but it would take time.

She moved around the center of the bay in a wide arc, looking for Rika and her team. She spotted Kelly first, slumped over a console, and then found Shoshin nearby. Both were in the same condition as Crunch and the fireteam at the door she'd entered. Then she spotted Rika, laid out on the command platform at Xa's feet.

"I don't care about the others. Dump them out the closest airlock, but this one comes with us back to Nietzschea."

His words lit a fire in Leslie, and she made a beeline for the spy who she realized had orchestrated so much of what had gone wrong over the past two weeks.

The spy who had destroyed the *Fury Lance*, and….

A minute later, she was standing at the edge of the command platform, her lightwand in hand. She crouched, coiling up her strength, before leaping into the air, her blade activating as she came down on Xa, ready to slice him from shoulder to groin.

Leslie was almost upon the smug-looking bastard, when a pulse blast hit her and she flew across the command platform and slammed into a console.

One of the Nietzschean spec-ops soldiers was in front of her a second later, railgun pointed at her head.

"Try something," he grunted. "I dare you."

* * * * *

<Niki! Why can't I see? …Or move?>

<Ri—>

A garbled thought came into her mind, and Rika wanted to scream—only she couldn't. She couldn't do anything other than think about how stupid she was for not coming into the bay lobbing grenades and razing it with her electron beam.

An eternity passed, and she began to wonder if maybe she was dying.

Maybe this is what happens when a mech dies. We don't see our past, or visions…just nothing. A nothing that fades into nothing.

<Well that was stupid, Rika.>

<Niki! Fuck! What was wrong with our Link?>

The AI gave a rueful laugh. *<Let's just say that I wish the ISF had rebuilt your biointerfaces.>*

<But a KK100 shouldn't have worked on us. We looked over the

one that Leslie captured.>

<*I guess Xa made some improvements. Either way, it only disabled your body control. It failed to properly sock-puppet you.*>

<*Nothing 'proper' about that. Did you fix our Link, then?*>

Niki didn't respond for a moment before saying, <*Uh…no, I activated another connection.*>

<*What other connection,*> Rika asked, half worried that the answer was what she thought it might be.

Nearly a year ago, Rika had tapped into abilities she'd never dreamed of possessing, a result of the L2 upgrades the ISF had performed on her brain. But Niki had told her later that, should Rika want to, a different path lay ahead of her, one not dissimilar to the road Tanis and Angela had taken when they merged into one being.

They'd spoken little of it since, and Rika hadn't concerned herself with it too much. Tanis and her AI had taken centuries to merge. Rika was usually more concerned with surviving the next week.

<*Let's talk about that later,*> Niki said. <*Suffice it to say that you're damn lucky that neither of us is normal.*>

<*Do we have any external senses?*> Rika asked, her statement a tacit agreement that they didn't need to discuss what a human-AI merge meant for them at that moment.

<*I should have access to the nanocloud I deployed right before we dropped. Working on bypassing the biolock too. Now that I see what they did, I'm reprogramming your interfaces. It might take some getting used to when you're back online.*>

<*Don't mess me up too much,*> Rika said. <*I'm going to need to hit hard and fast. I saw three other enemies right before I dropped.*>

<*Looks like more than that.*>

Rika's HUD came back online a moment later, and an overlay view of the bay appeared, showing Xa on the platform, with nine soldiers in various positions around the bay. Three were nearby, and she flagged those as her primary targets. Then Xa. Then it was a simple matter of cleanup.

<I'm ready,> Rika whispered. *<ETA?>*

<Five, four, three, two, one. Go!>

In an instant, Rika felt full control of her body come back. She swung her legs up and then down, flipping her body forward and landing on her feet. Somehow, her view of the bay felt sharper, so crisp that the edges of consoles and bulkheads hurt her eyes, like everything was too in-focus.

Ignoring the strange dissonance, she fired her GNR's electron beam, slicing off the arm of a soldier before spinning to fire on another. The third of the Niets on the platform was within reach, and Rika's left foot shot out, clamping onto her thigh and squeezing.

Her armor crumpled, and a muffled scream came from within the woman's helmet.

Rika ignored it and set her sights on Xa, his prior smug expression replaced by one of concern.

Curious, she thought. *Most people would show fear.*

She stepped forward and casually backhanded him—sending the unarmored man flying off the platform—while firing on another of the Nietzscheans.

A second later, a lightwand appeared in the air nearby. It hung above a Niet's head for a second before plunging through the man's helmet. A moment later it was gone, the falling corpse the only testament to the unseen attacker.

<Nice of you to join the party, Leslie,> Rika said.

<I was already dancing, they just made me sit one out. You OK?>

<Better than OK.>

Rika turned toward the entrance she'd come through, ignoring the rounds striking her body as she let loose with a barrage from her GNR, the weapon flinging kinetic bursts intermixed with electron beams. She shredded their cover and made her kill shots before jumping off the platform and striding toward Xa.

The Nietzschean spy was clawing his way up a console, something that was difficult with a broken arm.

"You're so lucky that I want to learn what you know," Rika muttered as she fought back the urge to kill the man where he stood.

"Good luck," Xa whispered. "I've faced off against far worse than you."

Rika laughed as Leslie signaled that her end of the bay was clear. The battle was won, though she feared the toll they'd find paid once the *Pinnacle* rose above Babylon's clouds.

"Yeah, I'm pretty nice. A lightweight, really. But you've not met Kora."

CLOUDTOPS

STELLAR DATE: 06.03.8950 (Adjusted Years)
LOCATION: GMS *Pinnacle,* Babylon
REGION: Genevia System, New Genevian Alliance

Rika stood at the Command Center with Chase at her side, the pair steering the ship out of the clouds.

Niki had disabled the KK100—after having it send a signal to release the mechs from their lockdown. Shortly afterward, Lieutenant Chris announced that the bridge was secured and the Niets there dead or wishing they were.

Leslie had taken her squad aft to find the engineers, whom one of the surviving Niets had said were still alive. Leslie had delivered the usual threats, and then taken Crunch's squad to find them.

Kelly, Keli, and Shoshin prowled the engineering bay, none of the three prepared to believe that they had fully secured the space until they'd stuck a rifle into every corner.

"You're making me anxious," Rika called out as Kelly stalked past.

"Me? You're the one standing up there with a big ol' bullseye on your back."

<*We're secure,*> Niki said on the team's net. <*I've filled this place with a nanocloud.*>

"That's great, Niki," Kelly said in a tone that implied anything but. "I'll just keep doing my manual sweep anyway."

<*Sure,*> the AI replied. <*Anything else you'd like to do the hard way, go for it. I hear you could cut down a tree and make paper to send a message to other people.*>

"Maybe I'll do that. It'll be quaint," Kelly shot back.

"We're almost through the clouds." Rika's words were clipped, and the others fell silent, Kelly turning to look at the large holodisplay on the forward bulkhead.

The ship's scan had picked up a field of small objects near the *Fury Lance*'s last known position. Rika had already steeled herself for the ship's destruction—though the confirmation on scan still hurt.

When the vessel had fired its DMG through the clouds, the ensuing lightning storm had damaged the forward sensor array. As such, they couldn't pick up any signals from beyond Babylon's stratosphere—especially not any that might have been emitted from escape craft.

She held her breath as they passed through the upper cloud deck, her hand finding Chase's as the rear sensor arrays were able to aim toward the debris field that was once Rika's pride and joy.

Goodbye, Lance.

<*I've got beacons!*> Niki shouted across the ship's general network. <*Three craft! Plus Piper!*>

Rika closed her eyes and drew a deep breath as the IDs of the survivors came up on the forward display.

Three craft meant that not all of the crew had made it.

"I knew every person on that ship," she said in a quiet voice that only Chase could hear.

"I know," he replied. "I did, too."

<*That better be you aboard that tub,*> Heather's voice came over Link a second later. <*Because I'm damn well sure that you owe me a ship right now.*>

<*It's gonna need a bit of work,*> Rika replied, a tear of relief tracing its way down her cheek.

<*Yeah, so did the* Lance. *You always give me the fixer-uppers.*>

<*I can give it to Vargo, if you'd prefer.*>

A gasp came from Heather. <*You* ***wouldn't****!*>

<*Heather,*> Rika's voice grew serious. <*Who didn't make it?*>

There was a pause before the *Lance*'s former captain responded. <*Bondo and Stripes.*>

"Dammit," Rika whispered, her throat constricting.

Suddenly, Niki laughed. *<Oh, I think they made it.>*

<How do you know that?> Heather asked, her earlier caustic tone gone.

<Because the Starcrusher just landed on our hull.>

<You have any openings?> Bondo's voice came over the shipnet a few seconds later. *<My last ship ran into a bit of engine trouble.>*

The man's words caused a dam to break open, and Rika found herself laughing and crying at the same time, until she couldn't breathe anymore. Chase's strong arm wrapped around her waist, and she sagged into him, finally catching her breath.

She looked up and saw his serious eyes above a knowing smile.

"You ready for whatever comes next?" he asked.

Rika drew in a deep breath, her shoulders surging up against the weight that rested on them. Somehow, the load felt lighter than it had over the past few weeks.

The ISF was gone, the enemy might have more DMG ships, and the *Fury Lance* had been destroyed. But they were still standing. The Genevian Marauders were just getting started.

"Yes. Yes I am."

THE END

* * * * *

Magnus Rika now commands the Genevian Marauders, but the Nietzscheans aren't going to let her rest on her laurels for long. With the ISF fleet gone, and the Marauders spread thin, it's the best time for the enemy to counterattack and halt

Rika's march toward Nietzschea.

Find out what happens next in ***Rika Coronated.***

MECH TYPES & ARMAMENTS

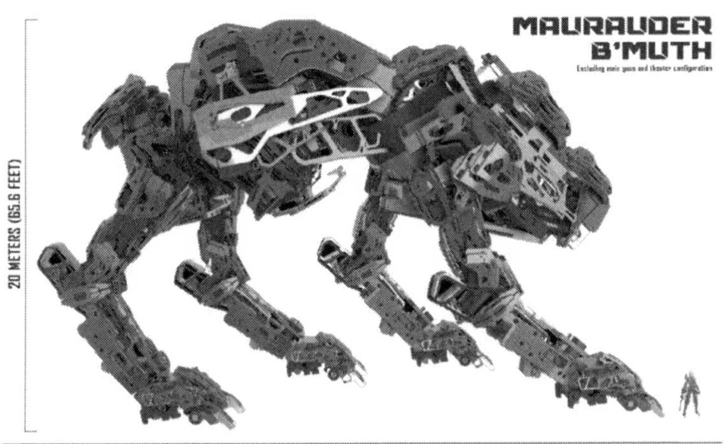

While these are the standard builds and configurations documented by the Genevian Armed Forces (GAF), many mechs reached the field in mismatched configuration, or were altered after deployment.

Sometimes these alterations were upgrades, sometimes downgrades, as repairs were often made with whatever spare components were available at the time.

The mechs in the Marauders generally align with the stated configurations, though many have altered themselves over the years.

NOTE: The K2R and all 4th generation models were made by Finaeus Tomlinson, in concert with Rika's Repair and

Maintenance team, specifically Lieutenant Carson and Corporal Stripes.

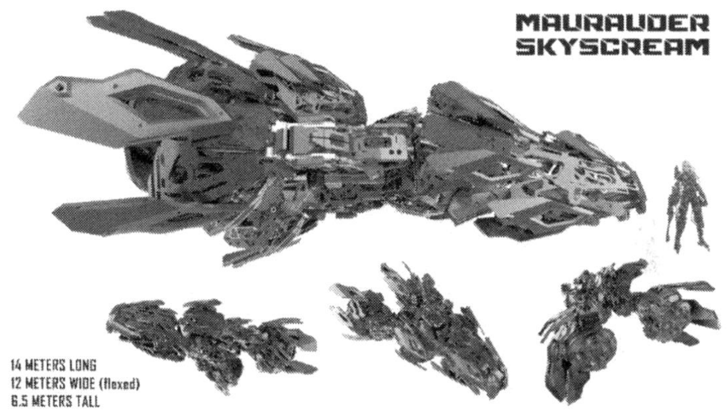

K1R (Kill Ranger – Generation 1)

This mech is more of a two-legged tank than a mech. The K1R sports a central 'pod' where the human is situated. None of the limbs utilize human material.

K1Rs often had mental issues due to feeling as though they had lost all sense of humanity. When the Nietzscheans won the war, they did not release any K1Rs from their internment camps. It is not known if they kept them, or killed them all.

Until the discovery of the mechs in the Politica, there was only a single K1R in the Marauders (who had been under General Mill's command at the end of the war). That mech has joined Rika's company to assist the four K1Rs Rika freed from the Politica in re-integration.

K1R mechs have a variety of heavy armament, including massive chainguns, railguns, missiles (with and without tactical nuke warheads), electron beams, and proton beams. They also sport a variety of suppression devices, from pulse, to sonic, to portable grav shields.

K1R mechs were not made later in the war, due to their cost and mental instability.

There were rumors that a limited run of K2R mechs were made, but no credible reports exist.

Sub-Models:

All K1R models could be outfitted with interchangeable armament, excepting the base model, which could not carry the tactical nukes.

K1R – The base K1R model was made in the early years of the war, and lacked the coordination and reactive armor of the later models.

K1R-M – The 'M' K1R added in the reactive armor, and included upgraded railguns with more advanced scan and target tracking systems. These mechs carried two missiles in launcher pods in their backs. They could be (and often were) upgraded to support the tactical nuke warheads on the missiles.

K1R-T – The 'T' model was a similar configuration to the 'M', but came standard with tactical nuclear warheads. Instead of the pair of launchers the K1R-M sported, the 'T' model carried as many as twelve missiles.

K1R-X-4 – 'M' and 'T' models both saw upgrades from Finaeus and the ISF engineers, which made them capable of functioning as AM or K1R models. None of the K1Rs opted to operate as AMs, but their 4th generation frames had considerable upgrades to power and armor. X-4 models have the ability to swap armament with AM models as well.

K2R-MBM – Based on designs Corporal Stripes stole at the end of the war, the K2R-MBM took the idea of a tank mech and raised the bar.

The Genevian military never had the energy to power their plans for the K2R mechs, but with miniaturized critical energy modules and ISF-grade SC batteries, the dreams of the GAF came into being under Finaeus's guidance.

The K2R-MBM is piloted by two AM-4 mechs (leveraging a part of the AM-T spec); one who manages movement and main-arm weapons, and another who controls the secondary arms, defensive systems, and secondary weapons systems.

On top of existing armament, the K2R-MBM brings to bear variable density proton beams, nanonet missiles, electron lashes, mortars (both thermite and HE), rapid-fire DPU cannons, as well as ground-hugger missiles.

The mech also functions as a re-armament center for its squad, and an attack drone deployment system.

AM (Assault Mech)

The AM mechs represented the bulk of the GAF's mechanized infantry program. It is estimated that over ten million AMs were created during the war, and over one hundred thousand are known to have survived. Many joined mercenary outfits or militaries of other nations.

AM model mechs were a 'torso-only' design, where none of the human's arms and legs were retained. The original idea was to make their cores swappable with K1R models, but it turned out that the mechanized infantry design of the AM models was generally more effective than the 'walking tank' design of the K1R models.

AM models were versatile mechs that had swappable loadouts. The improvements over time were mostly centered around human-mech integration, armor, and power systems.

AM mechs were often outfitted with chainguns, shoulder-mounted railguns, and electron beams.

Without known exception, AM mechs were always male.

Sub-Models

AM-1 – The original model of AM. Fewer than 100,000 AM-1 mechs were made, and none were known to have survived the war.

AM-2 – The AM-2 mechs quickly superseded the AM-1s, with better armor, more efficient power systems, and superior human-mech integrations.

AM-3 – The third generation of AM mech had upgraded power supply systems, and an artificial epidermis to remove the need for periodic removal and cleaning. Some AM-3s were also AI-capable.

AM-T – Design specs for AM-T mechs exist, but it is not known if any were made by the Genevians. The AM-T design utilized two AM-3 mechs working together in one larger body, controlling more limbs and separating motion and combat functions.

AM-4 – Designed by Finaeus Tomlinson, the AM-4 mechs are a step closer to humanity for the mechanized warriors. With stub limbs (like RR-3 and SMI models), the AM-4 mechs also utilize the MK99 chameleon armor epidermis.

AM-4s now support fully-swappable limbs with all other models, though they still possess the heaviest frames, and are capable of carrying heavier weapons, more ammunition, and heavier armor than any other mech type.

The 4th generation model now possesses internal, torso-mounted a-grav units for added mobility and stabilization.

RR (Recon/Ranger)

The RR model of mech was the precursor to the SMI model. RRs were based on both male and female humans, though smaller humans were used for RR models than AM and FR mechs.

These mechs were similar to AM models, except they were physically smaller and lighter. This allowed RRs to handle light aircraft/drop deployments.

As a compromise, they had smaller power sources, and could only operate for 2-3 days in the field.

Their loadouts were swappable with AM models, but they rarely utilized the chainguns.

Sub-Models

RR-1 – This model of mech began to appear on the battlefield around the same time as the AM-2 mechs. They utilized the power upgrade of the AM-2 mechs to have smaller power systems, but they also had a smaller power capacity. In theory, the new batteries of the AM-2 line should have worked, but they had overheating issues in the field, and more than one RR-1 had battery detonation when utilizing multiple firing systems.

RR-2 – The RR-2 mechs were rolled out around the same time as the AM-3s, and had few significant changes other than improved armor, and marginally longer-lasting power that no longer suffered from overload issues.

Second gen RR-2 mechs were also skinless, like AM-3 and SMI mechs.

RR-3 – The RR-3 mechs reached the field shortly before the end of the war, and were different in that they had partial legs, like SMI mechs. This was done as a cost/component-saving measure.

RR-4 – These mechs moved a step closer to the SMI spec, gaining the MK99 chameleon armor epidermis, and becoming lighter—even with their new stub limbs—thanks to advanced materials provided by the ISF.

The RR-4s use the same swappable weapons mounts as all mechs, but have high-output a-grav units in their thighs. These units allow them to fly at low altitudes (up to three hundred meters) and provide additional zero-*g* maneuvering options without using armor-based systems.

Seven of the RR-4s took the option for an additional set of arms and the brain modifications required to control the extra limbs.

FR (Force Recon)

Force Recon mechs were mechs that had the lighter drop capabilities of the RR mechs, with the additional power and armor of AM-3 models. All FR mechs were skinless.

Sub-Models

FR-1 – The first generation of FR mechs were limited run, and had both weight and power load distribution issues.

FR-2 – Second generation FR mechs solved many of the issues from the first generation, and were well regarded for their effectiveness.

XFR – The XFR model is not known to have been widely produced. This model had additional power and carrying capacity to utilize shoulder-mounted proton beams and chainguns. However, the mech's loadout made it almost as heavy as an AM-3 without the armor.

FR-4 – Though there is no FR-3 model, Finaeus and the members of Rika's Repair and Medical platoon decided to go with consistent generational numbering across all mechs.

The latest FR model gained the XFR's shoulder-mounted beam weapons: one an electron beam, and the other a high-output burst laser cannon. These weapons slot onto the wearer's back and slide up over the shoulder, where they are each capable of two-hundred-and-seventy-degree motion, even with the meter-long barrel on each.

Additional changes include a-grav stabilization similar to the AM-4s, and the same universal limb and weapons mounting system, as well as the MK99 chameleon epidermis.

SMI (Scout Mech-Integrated)

The final mech model produced at the end of the war was built out of a desire for a super-light mech that could be used in place of standard infantry in sniper/recon situations, and bring extreme fire to bear if desired.

SMI mechs were also cost-saving mechs, as they retained more of their human body components, making for fewer prosthetic neural connections. They also leveraged progress in muscle and bone augmentation that had been used in RR and FR mech models.

Mechs of this model were built exclusively from small, lithe women who could fit in the armor and still create a small profile.

Unlike other mech models, SMI mechs were never deployed with two functional hands. One was always a weapon mount.

SMI mechs are all skinless.

Sub-Models

SMI-1 – The first generation of SMI mechs had a short production run due to psychological issues. Because they retained more of their human bodies than other mechs, they ended up having additional dysphoria issues.

SMI-2 – Second generation SMI mechs had improved physical integrations and psychological conditioning that caused the mechs to view themselves as less human. However, in the field, it was observed to have the opposite effect, and SMI mechs retained a strong connection to their humanity.

SMI-3 – A few experimental SMI-3 models were produced near the end of the war. These models had more powerful legs and higher top speeds, and used a new short-barreled model of the GNR. Some SMI-3s were deployed with two GNRs and no 'regular' arm.

SMI-4 – Though there had always been rumors of an SMI-3, no one in the Marauders ever saw direct evidence that the model was produced. Still, for the same reasons as the FR-4s, the SMI range moved to '4' as well.

The SMI-4 mechs had few visible improvements to their configurations, excepting that they received the MK99 chameleon armor. Advanced materials shed over ten kilograms, while adding additional batteries and stronger bone and muscle enhancements. The SMI-4 armor also possesses the same chameleon capabilities as their skin.

While SMI-4s support the same universal weapons mount system as all mechs, they do not have the recoil control or power systems for some of the more powerful weapons, and stick to their tried and true rifles and GNRs.

LHO (Lateral Hyper Operation)

LHO mechs were a model created by Finaeus to suit the needs of shipboard operation in Rika's fleet. As the human crews within the 7th Marauder Fleet saw the skill and precision with which the ISF created the 4th Generation mechs, they began to request mechanization.

A problem the Marauder ships faced was that they were lightly crewed. To aid in solving this problem, Finaeus crafted a new mech body that was like an SMI in many respects, but possessed four arms and a slightly elongated torso. These mechs also had neural mods and brain alterations to handle operating a new set of limbs with full dexterity.

The desired—and achieved—result were mechanized humans capable of performing a taskload of two people. This ability created greater efficiency in the smaller crews, while also creating a formidable shipboard force to repel boarders if a ship were to come under attack while the bulk of its mechs were away on a mission.

The LHOs are all designated 4th Generation.

It should be noted that Finaeus had told Rika that 4-limbed mechs were not advisable due to the time it would take for their brains to learn how to manage the extra limbs.

This is why none of the LHO mechs have combat as a primary function, but are training for it. Some of the naval personnel who chose mechanization went for FR or SMI frames because they couldn't afford to take the time to learn how to manage extra limbs.

7th MARAUDER FLEET 1st DIVISION

This is a partial list and does not contain the full fleet roster.

Fleet Commander: Colonel Rika (SMI-4)
Fleet XO: Captain Heather (SMI-4)

Fury Lance
4100-meter dreadnought
420 fighters
Ship's AI: Piper
Captain: Captain Heather (SMI-4)
Navigation: Chief Warrant Officer Garth
Weapons and Scan: Chief Warrant Officer Ona
(Note: Ona and Garth frequently switch roles)

Republic IV
1100-meter cruiser
44 fighters
Ship's AI: N/A
Captain: Lieutenant Travis (AM-4)

Undaunted
1130-meter cruiser
34 fighters
Ship's AI: N/A
Captain: Lieutenant Ferris
Chief Engineer: Chief Warrant Officer Lara

Asora
544-meter destroyer
Ship's AI: N/A
Captain: Lieutenant Klen (RR-4)
Weapons and Scan: Chief Ashley (LHO-4)
Chief Engineer: Chief Glen

Capital
612-meter destroyer
Ship's AI: N/A
Captain: Lieutenant Buggsie

Dropship Pilots
- Chief Warrant Officer (CWO-3) Charles 'Mad Dog'
- Chief Warrant Officer (CWO-2) Halley

COLONEL BORDEN'S MARINES

Commanding Officer: Colonel Bartholomew Borden
Chief Rel – AI paired with Borden

Team 1 Leader: Lieutenant Saris
Team 1 Members:
- Sergeant Mona
- Corporal Pars
- Private Tina

Team 2 Leader: Lieutenant Gemma
Team 2 Members:
- Sergeant Daphne
- Private Kali
- Private Kev

9th MARAUDER BATTALION

After General Julia promoted Rika to Colonel and placed her in command of the 9th Battalion, Rika created 'N' Company, and moved two platoons into it. When the rest of the Marauders in her battalion arrived at Epsilon, she formed six more companies. Not all are listed below.

'HQ' COMPANY

Battalion Commander (CO): Colonel Rika (SMI-4)
Battalion Executive Officer (XO): Lieutenant Major Silva
Command Sergeant: Sergeant Major Barne (FR-4)
Operations Officer: Captain Niki (SAI)
Intelligence Officer: Captain Leslie

'R' COMPANY (M&M)

Platoon Commander – Lieutenant "Bondo" Carson
- Corporal Stripes (AM-X)

Other company commanders
Captain Meagan – SMI-4 (O Company)
Captain Gytra – RR-4-F (R Company)
Captain Crispin – K1R-4-X (S Company)
Captain Penelope – RR-4-F (T Company)

'M' COMPANY

Note, not all personnel in the Company are listed.

Company HQ

Commanding Officer (CO): Captain Chase (FR-4)
Executive Officer (XO): Lieutenant Karen (SMI-4)
First Sergeant: Tex (RR-4)
Gunnery Sergeant: Aaron (AM-4)
Tactics and Strategy AI: Potter

First Platoon

Platoon CO – First Lieutenant Chris (AM-4)
Platoon Sergeant – Staff Sergeant Kristian (RR-4-M)

First Squad
Sergeant Crunch (AM-4)
4 Fireteams (19 mechs)

FT 1-1
- CPL Ben (AM-4)
- PVT Al, 'Whispers' (AM-4)
- PVT Kim (RR-4-F)
- PVT Harris (FR-4)

FT 1-2
- CPL Kelly (SMI-4)
- PVT Shoshin (AM-4)
- PVT Keli (SMI-4)

FT 1-3

- PVT Kerry (RR-4)

FT 1-4
- CPL Mitch (RR-4)
- PVT Lauren (SMI-4)
- PVT Wolf (AM-4)
- PVT Matthew (AM-4)

Second Squad
Squad Sergeant – Corin (RF-4)
3 Fireteams (13 mechs)

FT 2-1
- CPL (K1R-X-4) Oosterwyk-Bruyn, 'The Van'
- PVT Ainsley (SMI-4)
- PVT Jenny (RR-4-F)

Third Squad
Squad Sergeant Carolyn 'CJ' (RR-4-F)
4 Fireteams (19 mechs)

FT 3-1
- PVT Kyle, 'Goob' (AM-4)
- CPL Yiaagaitia, 'Yig' (RR-4-M)
- PVT Cole (RR-4-F)
- PVT Fiona (SMI-4)

FT 3-2
- CPL Dave (AM-4)
- PVT Chad (FR-4)
- PVT Knight (AM-4)
- PVT Rouse (AM-4)

Fourth Squad

Squad Sergeant – Kara (SMI-4)
4 Fireteams (20 mechs)

Second Platoon

Platoon CO – First Lieutenant Fuller (AM-4)
Platoon Sergeant – Staff Sergeant Chauncy (FR-4)

Squad One
Squad Sergeant – Alison (SMI-4)
4 Fireteams (19 mechs)

FT 1-4
- CPL Fred (AM-4)
- PVT Jenisa (SMI-4)
- PVT Kor (AM-4)
- PVT Randy (AM-4)

Second Squad
Squad Sergeant – Tre (FR-4)
4 Fireteams (21 mechs)

Third Squad
Squad Sergeant Bean (SMI-4)
4 Fireteams (20 mechs)

FT 3-1
- CPL Hidee (SMI-4)

Fourth Squad
Squad Sergeant Kristina, 'Abs' (RR-4-F)
4 Fireteams (20 mechs)

FT 2-4
CPL Musel (AM-4)
PVT Bitty (K1R-X-4)
PVT Smitty (RR-4-F)

Third Platoon

Platoon CO – First Lieutenant Wilson (FR-4)
Platoon Sergeant – Staff Sergeant Bookie (SMI-4)

Squad One
Squad Sergeant Char (RR-4-F)
4 Fireteams (19 mechs)

Second Squad
Squad Sergeant Mal (FR-4)
4 Fireteams (22 mechs)

Third Squad
Squad Sergeant Cory (AM-4)
4 Fireteams (19 mechs)

Fourth Squad
Squad Sergeant Lana (SMI-4)
4 Fireteams (20 mechs)

'N' COMPANY

Note, not all personnel in the Company are listed.

Company HQ

Commanding Officer (CO): Captain Scarcliff (FR-4)
Executive Officer (XO): First Lieutenant Crudge (AM-4)
Gunnery Sergeant: Sergeant Johnny (FR-4)
Tactics and Strategy AI: Dredge

First Platoon

Platoon CO – First Lieutenant Michael (AM-4)
Platoon Sergeant – Staff Sergeant Alana (RR-4-F)

Squad One
Squad Sergeant Bruce (RR-4-M)
4 Fireteams (19 mechs)

Second Squad
Squad Sergeant Aerin (SMI-4)
4 Fireteams (21 mechs)

Third Squad
Squad Sergeant Justin (FR-4)
4 Fireteams (19 mechs)

Fourth Squad
Squad Sergeant Val (RR-4-F)
3 Fireteams (14 mechs)

Second Platoon

Platoon CO – Lieutenant Darla (RR-4-F)
Platoon Sergeant – Staff Sergeant Sal (FR-4)

Squad One
Squad Sergeant Sarah (RR-4-F)
4 Fireteams (19 mechs)

Second Squad
Squad Sergeant George (FR-4)
4 Fireteams (20 mechs)

Third Squad
Squad Sergeant Jessa (RR-4-F)
3 Fireteams (14 mechs)

Fourth Squad
Squad Sergeant Jynafer (RR-4-F)
3 Fireteams (13 mechs)

'Q' COMPANY

Note, not all personnel in the Company are listed.

Company HQ

Commanding Officer (CO): Captain Ron (AM-4)
Executive Officer (XO): First Lieutenant Bookie (SMI-4)

First Platoon

Platoon CO – First Lieutenant Layna (AM-4)
Platoon Sergeant – Staff Sergeant Boris (RR-4-F)

Squad One
Squad Sergeant Mela (RR-4-M)
4 Fireteams (19 mechs)

FT 1-1
Corporal Harlan (K1R-X-4)

THE BOOKS OF AEON 14

Keep up to date with what is releasing in Aeon 14 with the free Aeon 14 Reading Guide.

The Sentience Wars: Origins (Age of the Sentience Wars – w/James S. Aaron)
- Books 1-3 Omnibus: Lyssa's Rise

- Book 1: Lyssa's Dream
- Book 2: Lyssa's Run
- Book 3: Lyssa's Flight
- Book 4: Lyssa's Call
- Book 5: Lyssa's Flame

Legends of the Sentience Wars (Age of the Sentience Wars – w/James S. Aaron)
- Volume 1: The Proteus Bridge
- Volume 2: Vesta Burning

The Sentience Wars: Solar War 1 (Age of the Sentience Wars – w/James S. Aaron)
- Book 1: Eve of Destruction

Enfield Genesis (Age of the Sentience Wars – w/Lisa Richman)
- Book 1: Alpha Centauri
- Book 2: Proxima Centauri
- Book 3: Tau Ceti
- Book 4: Epsilon Eridani
- Book 5: Sirius

Origins of Destiny (The Age of Terra)
- Prequel: Storming the Norse Wind
- Prequel: Angel's Rise: The Huntress (available on Patreon)
- Book 1: Tanis Richards: Shore Leave
- Book 2: Tanis Richards: Masquerade

- Book 3: Tanis Richards: Blackest Night
- Book 4: Tanis Richards: Kill Shot

The Intrepid Saga (The Age of Terra)
- Book 1: Outsystem
- Book 2: A Path in the Darkness
- Book 3: Building Victoria

- The Intrepid Saga Omnibus – *Also contains Destiny Lost, book 1 of the Orion War series*

- Destiny Rising – *Special Author's Extended Edition comprised of both Outsystem and A Path in the Darkness with over 100 pages of new content.*

The Warlord (Before the Age of the Orion War)
- Books 1-3 Omnibus: The Warlord of Midditerra

- Book 1: The Woman Without a World
- Book 2: The Woman Who Seized an Empire
- Book 3: The Woman Who Lost Everything

The Orion War
- Books 1-3 Omnibus (includes Ignite the Stars anthology)

- Book 1: Destiny Lost
- Book 2: New Canaan
- Book 3: Orion Rising
- Book 4: The Scipio Alliance
- Book 5: Attack on Thebes
- Book 6: War on a Thousand Fronts
- Book 7: Precipice of Darkness
- Book 8: Airtha Ascendancy
- Book 9: The Orion Front
- Book 10: Starfire
- Book 11: Race Across Spacetime (2019)
- Book 12: Return to Sol (2019)

Building New Canaan (Age of the Orion War – w/J.J. Green)
- Book 1: Carthage
- Book 2: Tyre
- Book 3: Troy
- Book 4: Athens

Tales of the Orion War
- Book 1: Set the Galaxy on Fire
- Book 2: Ignite the Stars

Perilous Alliance (Age of the Orion War – w/Chris J. Pike)
- Book 1-3 Omnibus: Crisis in Silstrand

- Book 1: Close Proximity
- Book 2: Strike Vector
- Book 3: Collision Course
- Book 4: Impact Imminent
- Book 5: Critical Inertia
- Book 6: Impulse Shock

Rika's Marauders (Age of the Orion War)
- Book 1-3 Omnibus: Rika Activated

- Prequel: Rika Mechanized
- Book 1: Rika Outcast
- Book 2: Rika Redeemed
- Book 3: Rika Triumphant
- Book 4: Rika Commander
- Book 5: Rika Infiltrator
- Book 6: Rika Unleashed
- Book 7: Rika Conqueror

Non-Aeon 14 Anthologies containing Rika stories
- Bob's Bar Volume 2
- Backblast Area Clear

The Genevian Queen (Age of the Orion War)

- Book 1: Rika Rising
- Book 2: Rika Coronated (2019)
- Book 3: Rika Reigns (2019)

Perseus Gate (Age of the Orion War)
Season 1: Orion Space
- Episode 1: The Gate at the Grey Wolf Star
- Episode 2: The World at the Edge of Space
- Episode 3: The Dance on the Moons of Serenity
- Episode 4: The Last Bastion of Star City
- Episode 5: The Toll Road Between the Stars
- Episode 6: The Final Stroll on Perseus's Arm
- Eps 1-3 Omnibus: The Trail Through the Stars
- Eps 4-6 Omnibus: The Path Amongst the Clouds

Season 2: Inner Stars
- Episode 1: A Meeting of Bodies and Minds
- Episode 2: A Deception and a Promise Kept
- Episode 3: A Surreptitious Rescue of Friends and Foes
- Episode 4: A Victory and a Crushing Defeat
- Episode 5: A Trial and the Tribulations (2019)
- Episode 6: A Deal and a True Story Told (2019)
- Episode 7: A New Empire and An Old Ally (2019)
- Eps 1-3 Omnibus: A Siege and a Salvation from Enemies

Hand's Assassin (Age of the Orion War – w/T.G. Ayer)
- Book 1: Death Dealer
- Book 2: Death Mark (2019)

Machete System Bounty Hunter (Age of the Orion War – w/Zen DiPietro)
- Book 1: Hired Gun
- Book 2: Gunning for Trouble
- Book 3: With Guns Blazing

Fennington Station Murder Mysteries (Age of the Orion War)
- Book 1: Whole Latte Death (w/Chris J. Pike)

- Book 2: Cocoa Crush (w/Chris J. Pike)

The Empire (Age of the Orion War)
- Book 1: The Empress and the Ambassador
- Book 2: Consort of the Scorpion Empress (2019)
- Book 3: By the Empress's Command (2019)

The Sol Dissolution (The Age of Terra)
- Book 1: Venusian Uprising (2019)
- Book 2: Scattered Disk (2019)
- Book 3: Jovian Offensive (2019)
- Book 4: Fall of Terra (2019)

ABOUT THE AUTHOR

Michael Cooper likes to think of himself as a jack-of-all-trades (and hopes to become master of a few). When not writing, he can be found writing software, working in his shop at his latest carpentry project, or likely reading a book.

He shares his home with a precocious young girl, his wonderful wife (who also writes), two cats, a never-ending list of things he would like to build, and ideas…

Find out what's coming next at www.aeon14.com

Made in the USA
Columbia, SC
15 June 2019